# Through Many Dangers

## BOOK 2

The 25th Michigan infantry facing General John Hunt Morgan's cavalry at the Battle of Tebbs Bend, July 4, 1863. From *Illustrated Battles of the Nineteenth Century*, Volume 2. Cassell & Company, 1895.

# Through Many Dangers

## BOOK 2

## P.M. Kuiper

REFORMED
FREE PUBLISHING
ASSOCIATION

Reformed Free Publishing Association
Jenison, Michigan
© 2021 Reformed Free Publishing Association

All Bible quotations are taken from the King James [Authorized] Version

Reformed Free Publishing Association
1894 Georgetown Center Drive
Jenison MI 49428
616-457-5970
www.rfpa.org
mail@rfpa.org

Cover design by Erika Kiel
Interior design by Klaas Wolterstorff / KW Book Design

ISBN.    978-1-944555-89-4
ISBN.    978-1-944555-90-0 (ebook)
LCCN.    2021936575

# Contents

*"I have no news but this: the Rebels are about 3 to 4 miles away from here. What they are planning is known only to the Almighty God. We have to be prepared to leave at any moment. I would not be surprised if we will have to fight a hard-fought battle ..."*

Private Johannes van Lente
in a letter to his family, October 27, 1863

## CHAPTER 26

# SEPTEMBER – NOVEMBER 1863

Autumn arrived as the 25th Michigan marched over the rugged Cumberland mountain range on their way to Knoxville. Harm marveled at their beauty, at the great forested mountains with a thousand tumbling brooks and streams. He stopped to sketch them whenever he could. But marching through such terrain proved difficult.

After a difficult stream passage, Ted waded ashore to find the soles of his boots had not survived the crossing. He tied sheets of bark to his feet, but soon gave that up and went barefoot. The quartermaster had no boots at any price.

For several days, they marched in a driving rain. Then came suffocating heat and humidity. Food became scarce. Some of the soldiers fell behind on long marches. Others became too sick to continue. By the time they arrived in East Tennessee, they were a weary group. Short tempers boiled over into arguments and fights.

Colonel Moore gathered his brigade and announced that two members of each company would be allowed to travel home for a brief furlough. Kees volunteered. "My father runs a leatherworks company. I can arrange with him to bring back a load of boots."

"My mother's been sick with the ague," said Frank de Windt. "I should be allowed to see her before she dies."

Many argued that their families needed them to help with the harvest. Everyone made their case. All but Ted. Due to his strained relationship with his father, he preferred to stay in Tennessee.

In the end, Arend Boelema and Rinze Rietema were selected to go. Everyone liked them and wished them well, loading them down with messages for loved ones back home.

Harm and his friends discussed what it would be like for them. Every meal would be a celebration. Wherever they went, they'd be surrounded by people wanting to hear how the war progressed, how their boys were doing.

"And the best part," said Gerrit, "on Sunday they'll gather with the whole congregation to worship. What I wouldn't give to hear Rev. van Raalte open the word again."

Harm nodded in agreement.

The next morning, they continued their march toward Knoxville. It wasn't long before the old boredom set in. Charlie Marley held regular card games in his tent. Occasionally, Kees and Ted attended. Ted had managed to build quite a stack of dollars. But one night, he returned early from the game.

"What's wrong?" asked Harm.

Ted shrugged. "Turns out I won't be competing with Mr. de Groot to be the richest man in Holland."

"How much did you lose?"

"All of it."

"What happened?"

Ted sighed. "Some new recruit ran out of money but still wanted to play. He put a perfectly good pair of boots on the table. How could I resist? I thought I had them, too, with three queens. Turns out he had a full house."

Harm groaned.

"I know. The boots were my size, too."

The next day, they reached Knoxville. Just as they arrived in the area, the rebels pulled out of the city.

"They heard we were coming," said Kees. "They heard what we did to Morgan."

"They haven't gone far," said Captain de Boe. "Just down the road and across the river."

Kees raised his musket. "Let's go after them."

The captain shook his head. "Not yet. The river is swollen from the rains."

Colonel Moore set up camp on the banks of the Tennessee River directly opposite the rebels. Harm and Kees served picket duty on a bluff overlooking the river while rebel pickets guarded the other bank. From their post, Harm could see the campfires of both armies.

Kees found long nights on picket duty boring and livened them up by calling out to the rebels. "You've got no chance. Give up already."

Most nights they had the good sense to keep quiet. Other times, they'd curse Kees and the rest of the Yankees. Occasionally, Kees and the rebels would share a laugh at the incompetence of generals on both sides and the self-importance of minor officers everywhere.

One night, half a dozen rebel pickets bolted from their posts and splashed into the river.

"What's this?" said Kees.

Harm watched in amazement as they half-drifted, half-swam across the river.

"Cover me." Kees scrambled down the bluff to the water's edge.

A few minutes later, the rebels staggered ashore half-drowned. "What's the story, boys?" asked Kees.

"We've had enough." They were nearly naked, with no caps, bare feet, and rags for pants. They shivered in the cold and told how they hadn't eaten in a week.

Harm and Kees had precious little to eat themselves, but they set the rebels in front of a fire and shared their rations with them. When morning came, Harm and Kees led the rebels back to camp and delivered them to the stockade where they joined a growing number of rebel deserters.

Kees wagged his head. "Did you see their uniforms? It's embarrassing."

Harm pointed out that some in their own regiment still went barefoot.

Kees looked at Ted, whose feet were cracked and bloody from walking without boots. "That's not right."

Ted shrugged. "I check with the quartermaster every day. They don't have any boots."

"Somebody's got an extra pair," said Kees. "You know how officers hoard stuff. You got any money?"

Ted hung his head. "My experiment with gambling didn't end so well."

Kees turned to Harm. "You got anything worth trading?"

Harm's earthly possessions consisted of a Dutch psalm book and a King James Bible.

"A Bible for boots?" said Ted. "We wouldn't do *that* back home."

They asked around but failed to turn up a single soldier willing to part with his boots.

Ted was ready to give up, but Kees shook his head. "This isn't over." The next day, he brought it up again. "I've got an idea."

"Enough," said Ted. "There are no boots."

"Not in camp, maybe. But I have yet to see a farmer walking around with rags on his feet."

"Foraging?" asked Harm, doubtfully.

"This isn't Louisville. That was wrong. That was just sport. This is different. Ted needs boots. If he falls behind on a march, bushwhackers will get him."

Harm wished Gerrit was there to object to foraging, but Kees had made sure Gerrit was elsewhere before bringing it up.

"Look around," said Kees. "Everyone's doing it."

Harm sighed. He'd seen plenty of soldiers heading into the countryside to supplement their diet. Soldiers from Holland, too. The army wasn't able to feed them properly, and local farmers were in the middle of an abundant harvest.

"There's a war on," said Kees. "They're rebels."

"So were the Jemisons."

"We're not going to hurt anyone. It's just boots."

Harm wanted to hold his ground, but the sight of Ted's swollen and bruised feet made it hard. The danger of bushwhackers was too real to ignore.

They slipped out of camp and made their way to a nearby farmhouse with several large barns. As they approached the house, Kees attached his bayonet.

Harm stepped in front of him. "You said we weren't going to hurt anyone."

"Of course not." Kees brushed past him. "This is just to focus their attention." He knocked on the door.

A farmer appeared in the doorway, a large man with leathery skin reddened from the sun.

Kees addressed him, "We're here to give you an opportunity to volunteer a pair of boots to the cause of freedom."

7

The farmer looked at Ted's feet, then back at Kees. "I wish I could help you, but I don't have any boots to spare."

"The thing is," said Kees, "we're not looking for a *spare* pair."

The farmer glared at them through steel gray eyes. His brow furrowed as he took note of Kees' bayonet, then turned to his own boots. "Perhaps . . . I could part with these."

"Perhaps you should."

He removed his boots, never taking his eyes off Kees. His socks needed darning. He handed the boots to Kees, who handed them to Ted.

"Thank you kindly," said Kees. "Now, about your smokehouse."

The farmer's lips tightened.

"We haven't had a proper meal in a month. Mind if we take a bit of ham with us?"

Through clenched teeth, the farmer muttered, "Help yourself."

Outside, Kees made his way toward the smokehouse.

"Boots are one thing," said Harm. "Anything else is just thievery."

"He's got plenty."

"Doesn't matter."

"He's a rebel."

"Doesn't matter."

"I asked nicely." Kees entered the smokehouse and reappeared a minute later with a thick ham speared on the end of his bayonet.

Back at camp, they sat down to a rare feast. Hungry as he was, Harm excused himself and walked down by the creek to do his laundry.

Spencer spotted him and splashed over to join him. "Stop by my tent tomorrow. I got my hands on a harmonica."

"I'd love to," said Harm, "but I doubt I'll have time. We drill morning, noon, and night."

"I know. But you'll like this. Willem, too. You could report sick. I'll do the same. We'll lay low for a couple of hours, then make a miraculous recovery."

Harm was tempted, but shook his head. "We could go into battle any day. It wouldn't be right to skip drill."

Spencer smiled. "Still concerned with right and wrong, huh?"

Harm dropped his eyes, embarrassed.

"I thought maybe you'd given that up. I've noticed the boys from Holland forage as well as anyone."

Harm looked up, startled. His face flushed.

"I'm sorry," said Spencer. "That was one of the issues I had with my parents. They talked one way and acted the opposite. You know, hypocrites. But I didn't mean to suggest you'd do that."

Harm looked away. "It's not . . . I'm sorry, I have to go."

That night, Harm couldn't sleep. Was he a hypocrite? He knew stealing was wrong. But without boots, Ted might fall behind on a march and be killed. He prayed, but his words felt cold. How could he ask forgiveness when he might do the same thing the next day?

Not long after, Kees asked Harm, "What are you doing tonight?"

Harm held up a hand. "No more foraging."

"No. Of course not. And taking that ham the other night was wrong. I'm sorry about that. You should have stopped me."

Harm didn't respond. He knew from experience how difficult it was to stop Kees when his mind was set on something.

He feared Kees might begin regular foraging raids after that. But Kees didn't mention it again even though they often went hungry.

Over the next several days, the rains came to an end and the river levels began to fall. Colonel Moore ordered the brigade to cross over and engage the rebels on the other side. The fighting was limited to the forward skirmish line. Harm and his friends marched near the middle of the brigade and never fired their weapons. The rebels put up an hour's resistance, then fell back.

After several days of retreat, the rebels stiffened their defenses, then mounted an assault of their own, pushing Colonel Moore's brigade back. This time, the fighting was limited to the rear guard as the Union forces retreated. The two armies ended up in their original positions, facing each other across the river. The pattern repeated itself again the next week.

"What's the point?" complained Gerrit. "It's like they can't justify feeding us if we don't engage the enemy."

"But they *don't* feed us," said Ted.

"We should do more than engage them," said Kees. "We need to sustain an attack. Drive them back where they came from."

"We're in Tennessee," said Ted. "This *is* where they came from."

Harm was just glad they'd avoided the fighting. He worried that Owen or Blake Jemison might be among the rebel soldiers. And even if they weren't, surely other rebel soldiers had mothers and sisters that loved them.

Back in camp, Kees grew bored again. "There's a card game tonight over at Charlie Marley's. I thought maybe you'd give it another chance."

Harm shook his head. "No thanks."

Kees turned to Ted. "How about it?"

Ted sighed. "I'll pass."

"Are you sure? I can loan you $20 to get you back in the game."

Ted eyed the money.

"You don't have to pay me back right away," said Kees. "I can wait until we get paid again."

Ted hesitated, then shook his head. "No thanks."

"You sure?"

He nodded. "I'm with Gerrit now—work for my bread and avoid vain persons."

A few days later and in the midst of the fighting, the army decided to remove Colonel Moore from command. Harm was stunned. No explanations were given, but rumors swept through camp. Most blamed General Boyle.

"He still holds a grudge against Colonel Moore," said Kees.

Colonel Mott of the 118th Ohio took over the brigade. Under his command, the same pattern persisted. They would advance a few days, then retreat as the rebels pushed back.

In late October, by rotation, the 25th Michigan took their turn at the lead in one of those advances. Harm and his friends formed the forward skirmish line.

"We've got nothing to fear," said Kees. "Remember what we did to General Morgan at Tebbs Bend."

Harm didn't respond. This time *they* were attacking, while the *rebels* were dug in behind defensive works.

They spread out ten feet apart and advanced. Harm fired into the rebel line and dropped to a knee to reload. The rebels hid behind boulders and fallen trees and poured musket fire into the advancing troops. The noise was fearsome.

Harm moved forward, firing and reloading. Rebel muskets crackled angrily and a ball whined past just inches from his head. Smoke drifted lazily between the lines, refusing to dissipate. The scent of gunpowder hung heavy in the air.

Captain de Boe urged them forward. "We're not here to trade fire. Advance."

Harm and his friends moved forward. The rebel muskets grew louder and fiercer as the distance between the lines diminished. Slivers of bark and splintered stones sliced through the air. Harm stumbled and landed hard on his shoulder. Balls buzzed overhead like hornets. He rose to his feet and continued on.

One by one, the rebels gave up their positions and began to fall back. Harm pushed on, scrambling over rocks and logs, firing into the rear guard of the retreating rebels. Off to his left he heard someone cry out, but couldn't determine if it was a fallen rebel, or one of his own company.

Eventually, the rebels gave up firing and simply fled. Harm and his company pursued them, but relaxed as the resistance melted away. The sun angled through the canopy of trees. Harm enjoyed the sharp scent of apples in the air and the crunch of golden leaves underfoot. It reminded him of walking in the woods back home, except that he'd nearly been killed an hour earlier.

Thinking of home got Harm thinking about Sarah. He decided to write her again as soon as he got back to camp and let her know he missed their talks.

When the sun set behind the low hills, Captain de Boe ordered them to halt. They set up camp on a creek near the city of Louden. Harm and Ted went down to the creek to gather water. When they returned, Kees asked, "Do you know who was injured? I heard someone cry out."

"I heard it, too," said Harm. "I hoped it was a rebel."

Kees shook his head. "I don't think so. It was one of us."

## CHAPTER 27

# NOVEMBER 1863

Harm looked around in alarm. "Who's missing? Where's Gerrit?"

No one could remember seeing Gerrit since morning. Harm frantically searched for him among the tents. Finally, he checked with Captain de Boe.

"Gerrit's accounted for. He's on picket duty."

Harm breathed a sigh of relief and returned to the fire.

"Who then?" wondered Kees. "Willem?" Again, panic rose in Harm's chest.

"Follow me," said Kees. "We'll check the hospital."

The regimental hospital was a makeshift tent a half-mile behind the line. Harm prayed the whole way there. How could he return to Holland without his cousin? Uncle Ben would be heartbroken. And what of Aunt Nel?

At the hospital, two surgeons stood in lamplight, feverishly working over a soldier. Harm couldn't bear to look. Kees stepped under the tent and conferred with a guard. When he returned, he said, "That's not Willem. He was here earlier, but he's over at the brigade hospital now."

The brigade hospital operated out of an abandoned house near the river. Again, Harm prayed, but this time resentment crept in. Why Willem? He'd volunteered for extra duty all the time and never caused trouble. Why would God take him when others shirked their duty and brought shame to their uniform? Why should Holland lose someone with so much potential?

Harm's chest grew tight as he approached the brigade hospital. What if they found Willem laid out on a table like Arie Rot? Or strapped to a bed, fighting for his life?

Instead, they found him sitting at a table, drinking coffee. "Willem!"

Willem rose in surprise. "What are you doing here?"

"Looking for you," said Kees, "We thought you were hurt."

"Me? No, I'm all right."

"What are you doing here?" asked Harm.

"I helped carry Howard."

Howard! Harm's heart nearly stopped. "Where is he?"

"They're still working on him."

"How bad is it?"

Willem pointed to a spot low on his right side. "It went right through. An inch lower and it would have shattered his hip."

The door swung open and a surgeon joined them. "We've patched him up, but he's lost a lot of blood."

"Can we see him?" asked Harm.

"Not anymore today. Come back tomorrow."

Harm was scheduled for guard duty the next day, but Kees agreed to take his shift. Harm returned to the hospital with Ted. They found Howard resting in a bed, his entire midsection wrapped in bandages. He opened his eyes when they entered the room and tried to raise himself, but winced and fell back. "It doesn't hurt if I don't move."

"What happened?" asked Ted. "How'd you get hit?"

Howard shrugged. "I don't know. I stepped over a log and felt a stab of pain in my side. I don't remember anything after that. I woke up here."

"How bad is it?" asked Ted.

Howard shrugged. "The surgeon told me I was lucky."

"No broken bones. It could have been a lot worse."

"Yeah. I guess. But it doesn't feel so good." He asked them to pray with him.

Harm prayed that Howard's injury would soon heal and God would use doctors and hospitals and medicines to restore him to strength. He swallowed hard and concluded, "if it be thy will."

Howard opened his eyes. "Thank you. I've been thinking about God's will. He has a purpose for each of us, right?"

Harm nodded.

"What if I'd been killed today? I haven't done anything."

"You have," said Harm. "You don't have to be some kind of hero."

"I should have done *something* though. I should have changed the world somehow. God didn't put me here to just take up space."

"It's hard to change the world from Holland," said Ted.

Howard smiled. "Look at Rev. van Raalte, though. He did something."

"We each do our part," said Harm. "We can't all be like Rev. van Raalte."

"Gerrit can," said Ted, "but not all of us."

Howard held his side and groaned. "Don't make me laugh. It hurts too much."

"Look at your father," said Harm. "He may not change the world, but he goes out every day and works the fields. He feeds his family and raises his children."

Howard looked grim. "I went and joined the army instead."

"That's service, too. Honor and duty and all that."

Howard sighed. "Don't make it sound noble. I didn't join out of some higher calling. I just didn't want to look like a coward."

"You think you're the only one?"

"I know. But sometimes I wonder if I've ever done *anything* that wasn't motivated by pride or self-interest." He paused. "You think we should have stayed home?"

Harm hesitated. "I think . . . the important thing now is that we live faithfully while we're here."

"Which you did," said Ted. "Advancing on a line of ill-tempered rebels wasn't exactly self-interest."

Howard sighed. "Lot of good it did."

"Who knows," said Harm. "Maybe God will use our service to save the Union."

"Maybe?"

"If that's his will."

"Ah, his will again."

"It's no different back home. We work the fields, but God sends the sun and rain. He gives the harvest."

"Except when he doesn't," said Ted.

Howard nodded. "His ways are higher than our ways. I know that. I guess I just need to accept it."

"It's the same with Rev. van Raalte. He preaches. He teaches. But he can't save anyone. Only God can change a heart."

"And he doesn't always do that," said Ted.

Howard managed to raise himself up a bit. "My father says, 'ora et labora.' It's Latin, I think, 'pray and work.' We begin with prayer because God is God; He can accomplish anything. But then we work, too, with all our strength, because that's a means God uses to accomplish things."

Harm nodded. "That sounds right. If we pray and refuse to

work, we tempt God. If we work and forget to pray, we imagine we can do things in our own strength."

"Don't get me wrong." Howard said, readjusting his position in the hospital bed. "I wouldn't want to stand on anything I've done. We're saved in Jesus' blood. That's enough. I just wish I'd shown more gratitude."

"We all do," agreed Harm.

"Would you do something for me?" Howard turned to face Harm. "Would you write my family and let them know what happened?"

"Of course."

A surgeon entered the room to check on Howard. He wanted to change Howard's dressing and suggested Harm and Ted head back to camp.

"We'll come back tomorrow," said Harm.

"Don't bother," said the surgeon. "He's scheduled to be transferred to a hospital in Knoxville."

"Is that necessary?" asked Harm.

"It's for the best. He'll get better care there."

As Harm walked back to camp, he realized how much he'd miss Howard. Back in Holland, Howard had merely been Sarah's brother. Now, it seemed, they were friends.

Back at his tent, Harm wrote a difficult letter to Howard's family. He wrote about the battle, Howard's injury, and his transfer to the hospital in Knoxville. He made sure to mention Howard's faith. His family would want to know that.

He read what he'd written and decided it sounded too dark. Talk of Howard's faith made it sound like he was hurt worse than he actually was. Harm concluded the letter by assuring them he'd be all right.

When he returned from delivering the letter to the postmaster, he found the camp humming with excitement. Arend Boelema and Rinze Rietema had returned from their furlough. Everyone gathered around, peppering them with questions about home.

"How is Rev. van Raalte?" asked Gerrit.

"He was sick for a long time, but he's better now," answered Arend.

"He reads all the papers and follows the progress of the war," added Rinze. "He can list every battle. He even follows the scheming in Washington and the draft riots in New York City. Of course, he knows all about our company."

"How was church?" asked another.

"So good," said Arend. "The prayers and the singing. They even celebrated communion while we were there. Rev. van Raalte remembers us in his congregational prayers."

Talk of home filled Harm with a longing to return. He'd been gone over a year. How much longer?

"How about the city?" asked Willem. "Has it changed?"

"It's growing," said Rinze. "Lots of new buildings. Eighth Street has more stores than ever. Lots of Americans, too."

The next day, Harm had a chance to talk to Rinze privately. Rinze assured him his family was well. "Sam has grown up so much. Trina, too. I'm afraid your father's still a copperhead, though."

Harm looked up, surprised, but didn't reply. He knew better. Copperheads were Northerners who held Southern sympathies. His father had no sympathies for North *or* South. He only had sympathies for his family and for the church.

"I think we can count on Sam, though," said Rinze.

"Sam?"

"When he turns eighteen, I'm sure he'll volunteer."

The shock took Harm's breath away. How could Sam even think of it?

Harm complained about it to Kees, but got no sympathy. "We could use him," said Kees. "He'll make a good soldier."

"He's needed at home."

"We're all needed at home. We're needed here, too."

Harm stormed off to write Sam a letter. It ran three pages. If he'd had more paper, it would have run seven. He told Sam how foolish it would be for him to run off to war. He had no idea what dangers it held. Boys like him died every day. Americans thought nothing of breaking God's commands. Some from Holland were no better. And besides, Father couldn't run the farm alone. The family would starve. On the way to the postmaster, Harm thought of more arguments and scribbled them across the back of the envelope.

## CHAPTER 28

# NOVEMBER 1863

A crisp autumn breeze swept the last of the maple leaves across the yard in front of the van Wyke home.

Father set up the big ladder, and Sam climbed onto the roof of the barn to make sure the shingles were in good shape for the coming winter. Mother spent the morning washing and peeling apples for applesauce. Trina helped stir. Soon the house smelled of cinnamon and vanilla.

Later, Sam went to town to work on a school project together with his friends. Father asked him to run a couple of errands in town and also check at the post office. He received two letters from Harm, one addressed to himself and one to his family. He read the one addressed to himself, put the other in his pocket, and set off for home.

Trina took her dolls to play in the grass by the lane. From there she could see Sam the moment he returned over the hill. She felt sure he would return with a letter from Harm.

Sam didn't keep her in suspense. As soon as he saw her, he pulled the envelope out of his pocket and waved it in the air. Later, Father came in from burning some brush. His shirt was flecked with ash and he smelled of wood smoke. He saw Harm's letter on the table and gathered the family.

———

Louden, Tennessee
November 9, 1863
Dear Father, Mother, and family at home,
The rattle of muskets still echoes in my ears! For weeks the armies of North and South have dodged and feinted at each other. We have marched often and fought little. That changed yesterday. We marched at the front of the brigade and took heavy fire. Musket balls buzzed about like hornets. I was plenty frightened until the rebels took our suggestion and retreated.

I can say with gratitude that I am unharmed and in good health. I pray that you are healthy as well.

———

Father stopped reading. The color had drained from Mother's face. "Winter is coming," he said. "If it's a cold one, the fighting will stop. Both sides will stay in camp and try to stay warm and dry."

"We'll pray for a cold winter, then," said Mother.

Father smiled and turned back to the letter,

———

I'm sorry to say, Howard Tillema is among the injured. A musket ball struck him in the side. Thankfully, he has no broken bones. Ted and I just visited him. He's in good spirits and spiritually strong. He'll soon go to the hospital in Knoxville. I don't know when we'll see him again. Keep Howard in your prayers. His family too. I have written them.

Mother's hand went to her face at the first mention of Howard's injury, and stayed there when Father stopped reading.

"I'm sure he'll be all right," said Father, looking up. "Harm would have told us if it was serious."

Arend and Rinze returned to camp with wonderful tales of home. We envy their time in Holland. Rinze told me he enjoyed his time with you very much. He called it "true hospitality."

Sam, I wrote you a letter earlier today so I will not repeat that here.

Father stopped and looked at Sam. "You got a letter from Harm?"

Sam looked embarrassed.

"Today? You weren't going to tell us?"

"I thought . . . I didn't . . ."

"Perhaps it wasn't meant to be shared," said Mother quietly.

"Oh." Father stopped. "All right, then."

"It's not a big secret," said Sam. "He just . . . Rinze told him I was planning to enlist. Harm suggested I reconsider."

"You're planning to enlist?" Father's voice was steady, but the veins in his neck bulged.

"No."

"Where would Rinze get an idea like that?"

"Rinze tried to talk me into it. Honest. I didn't say I would."

"How about the *dominie*? Has he talked to you as well?"

"No. I mean, he talks about the war all the time. But he didn't tell me to enlist."

Father turned back to the letter. "Very well. We'll read our letter and leave Sam's letter to Sam."

———

Trina, I drew a picture of trees reflected in the waters of the Tennessee River. I wish I could have captured their autumn col-

THROUGH MANY DANGERS 2

ors, gold and deep orange. Since I don't have brushes and oils, you'll have to use your imagination.

---

Father removed the picture and held it up so the others could see it.

"That's a good one," said Sam. "It reminds me of the one he painted for Anna just before he left."

"I wish mine had colors," said Trina. She studied it longer. "It is pretty, though. I can almost see the colors."

Father turned back to the letter,

---

We are camped on the banks of the Tennessee River not far from Knoxville. The rebels are camped directly across the river from us. I can see their campfires from where I stand.

I am thankful you enjoyed another plentiful harvest and pray for continued blessings for you through the coming winter. As for us, we await God's will.

Your loving son and brother, Harm VanWyke

---

Much later, in front of the fire, Mother said, "You noticed how he spells his name now?"

Father sighed. "I noticed."

## CHAPTER 29

# NOVEMBER 1863

At drill, Harm learned that Howard had not yet been transferred to the hospital at Knoxville. He was still in the brigade hospital. That evening, he went to see him.

"Hey," said Harm. "I thought you'd be in Knoxville by now."

"I know," said Howard. "They were expecting an ambulance yesterday, but some general re-directed it. They're hoping for another later today."

Harm was happy for the chance to visit Howard again. He told him about Arend and Rinze returning. Howard listened intently. "I'm glad Rev. van Raalte is better."

They talked of home and church and what they would do after the war. Howard thought he might go into his uncle's wagon-making business. Harm admitted he wasn't sure what he'd do. Probably farm like his father.

"Sarah will be happy to see you," said Howard.

Harm's face grew warm. "It's been over a year. I'm not sure . . ."

"She asks about you all the time."

"I've thought of writing her but I don't want to seem . . ."

"She'd like that."

"Maybe after the war . . ."

"She'd like that."

After an hour and a half, the surgeon interrupted them, suggesting Harm let Howard get his rest.

Harm rose to go. "Oh, I wrote your family."

"Thank you."

When Harm returned to camp, he found it a whirlwind of activity. Soldiers rushed about, striking tents, loading wagons, and packing up gear. Harm flagged down Captain de Boe. "What's going on?"

"The rebels are pushing in this direction. We have orders to fall back to Kingston."

"When?"

"Now."

"What about Howard? He's still at the brigade hospital."

"They'll get him out by ambulance, I expect."

"They don't have any. They were just complaining about it."

The captain shrugged. "There's nothing we can do."

Harm joined the columns and marched away from Louden, away from the hospital, and away from Howard. Darkness descended, and still they marched. Well after midnight, they came to a halt. Colonel Mott established a new camp on the banks of the Clinch River outside Kingston.

Harm and his friends set up their tents and collapsed in exhaustion. Hours later, Harm awoke with one thought. What had become of Howard?

"The rebels took Louden," said Captain de Boe. "The surgeons got out, and some of the injured, but Howard was too weak to travel."

Harm thought he was going to be ill. He'd heard stories of Confederate prison camps, soldiers sleeping outdoors with no shelter and no clean water. Disease and starvation. For Howard's sake, he forced himself to hold out hope. The camps *couldn't* be as bad as they said.

Harm realized he'd have to write Howard's family again, letting them know what had happened. He stared at a blank sheet of paper for a long time. What could he write? He'd assured them Howard would be all right and now he wasn't. They'd hate him. Sarah too.

He had to do something. But what?

The rebels took courage from their success at Loudon and marched on toward Kingston.

"It's General Wheeler," said Captain de Boe, "with six thousand men."

Harm remembered that name. Owen Jemison served with General Wheeler.

Kees sighed. "Out-numbered again. I wish we had Colonel Moore back."

"Don't worry," said a soldier from the 118th Ohio. "Colonel Mott has gotten us out of more than one scrape."

Colonel Mott ordered every soldier in his brigade to spread out in a long skirmish line. It snaked through fields and forests for nearly two miles.

"Everyone on the skirmish line?" said Kees, doubtfully. "No main line? No reserve? The rebels will punch right through."

The boys from Holland took their place in a stand of tall pines. They chopped down trees and reinforced the gaps to form rough defensive works.

As they waited for the rebels to arrive, Harm's mind wandered back to Howard. A rescue plan formed in his mind. If he allowed himself to be captured, maybe the rebels would bring him wherever they held Howard. Then he could help Howard escape. He took a chance, and mentioned the plan to Kees.

"Too risky," said Kees.

"We have to do something."

"We will."

Before Harm could ask him what he had in mind, a line of rebel skirmishers appeared some fifty yards out. The morning quiet was shattered as a hundred muskets fired.

Harm eased his musket forward and fired into the advancing soldiers, then ducked behind the works and reloaded. Musket balls pelted the trees around him.

A rebel in bare feet stepped out from behind a tree and fired into the works, then ducked behind the tree again. Kees waited for him to reload and was ready when he reappeared. The rebel fell against the pine tree and slid to the ground.

The skirmishing continued throughout the morning. Then, with the sun high in the sky, it ended almost as suddenly as it had begun. The firing became sporadic. It moved further down the line, and then died out entirely.

Stepping out from behind his works, Harm saw the barefoot rebel soldier twisted at the base of the tall pine. He was only a boy, no older than fifteen years. Harm looked away as a shiver ran down his back. How old was Owen Jemison?

Back in camp, they learned the rebels had turned back and retreated to Louden.

"Why?" asked Kees. "They outnumbered us two to one. They could have punched through anywhere they wanted."

"They didn't know that," said Willem. "They probed all along our skirmish line and assumed we'd have three times as many waiting behind."

Kees scratched his chin. "Maybe this new colonel *does* know a thing or two."

Everyone was excited after the successful defense of Kingston. They gathered around the fires, celebrating their victory. But Harm couldn't bring himself to join in. The thought of Howard in enemy hands was too awful.

Kees found him brooding in his tent and asked, "What are you doing tonight?"

Harm didn't answer.

"Interested in slipping out of camp?"

"Foraging? No."

Kees lowered his voice. "I thought you and I could slip over to Loudon and see about Howard."

Harm looked up. "What's the point? They've transferred him to a prison camp by now."

"Maybe. But he's injured. Maybe they haven't moved him yet."

Harm stepped closer. "Tell me more."

"It won't be easy."

"Just the two of us?"

"It's too dangerous to involve anyone else."

It was true. They'd have to go behind rebel lines. Their chances of success were slim. But Harm *had* to do it. For Sarah. For Howard. "Why would *you* risk it?" he asked Kees. "You hardly know Howard."

Kees grinned. "I'm not doing it for him. Let's go before I change my mind."

They stood for roll call, then slipped out of camp and hurried down the pike toward Louden. Harm took comfort as darkness fell. The only way their plan could work was complete surprise. If they were discovered at any point, they'd end up prisoners just like Howard.

But as the last shreds of light faded in the western sky, Harm grew tense. The night sounds felt somehow sinister and foreboding.

Kees came to a sudden halt. "I hear voices."

Harm thought he heard them, too. But when they listened more carefully, they couldn't make out anything distinct. A half hour later, they thought they heard the creak of a wagon approaching on the road. Then, the sound of pursuing dogs. By the time they approached Loudon, Harm was mentally and physically exhausted.

The two left the road as they approached a line of pickets outside the rebel camp. Kees crawled toward the line on his belly, popping up occasionally to get a better look. He stopped under a huge chestnut tree at the edge of a small green pond. "They're making it easy. They put their pickets in all of the same places we used when we held Loudon."

They continued on, crawling through a gap in the rebel line. Soon, they crouched in the shadows outside the hospital. Two soldiers stood guard at the front door. Several stretchers lay in the yard. A hand cart leaned against the house.

"I'll go down by the river and draw their fire," said Kees. "Don't worry. I'll be fine. You sneak in and get Howard."

"All right," said Harm. "We can meet back at that big chestnut tree."

"Right . . . uh . . . which one was that again?"

"The chestnut. Where we stopped before. By the pond."

"Oh. *That* chestnut." He grinned and slipped away.

Harm remained crouched in the shadows.

Five minutes later, the crack of Kees' musket snapped the guards to attention. They spoke excitedly, then raced off in the direction of the river.

Harm emerged from the shadows and crept toward the hospital, making a mental note of the location of the stretchers and the hand cart. Suddenly, three more soldiers burst out from the hospital. Harm fell to the ground, afraid to move. The soldiers argued amongst themselves, then followed the guards toward the river. Harm raced to the hospital and stepped inside, his heart pounding. Howard was still in the same room, but something had changed. His hair was matted with perspiration and his breath came in raspy gasps.

Harm touched his arm. His skin felt hot. "Howard?"

"What?" Howard opened his eyes. He licked his lips and tried to say more.

"Shhh." Harm motioned for him to keep quiet. "We've come to get you out of here."

Howard's eyes widened, but he said nothing.

"What did they do to you?"

"They didn't . . ." His voice broke off and he gasped for breath. "They tried to help, but . . ."

The door to the room opened and a rebel surgeon appeared. He recognized Harm's uniform and tried to back away, but Harm grabbed him and pulled him into the room. "I'm taking Howard back with me."

The surgeon looked doubtful. "He's in no shape for a journey. He may not survive it."

"Will he survive here?"

The surgeon dropped his eyes.

Harm moved to Howard's side and tried to raise him from the bed. He realized how difficult moving him was going to be. He turned to the surgeon. "Help me."

After a moment of indecision, the surgeon joined him. Together, they lifted Howard and carried him to the door. Howard grimaced in pain, then lost consciousness entirely.

Outside, they placed him in the box of the hand cart. One of his arms hung over one side of the box and both feet stuck out the other side, but there was no time to do more. Harm grabbed the two long handles of the cart and wheeled Howard toward the woods. The surgeon called after him, "I'm sorry. I truly am."

Harm reached the woods but found the cart almost impossible to manage. He could have moved faster by throwing Howard over his shoulder, but worried about reopening the wound. He continued on, dragging the cart over rocks and fallen branches.

As he wrestled it down the bank of a narrow creek bed, the cart tipped dangerously. One wheel sunk into a pool of oozing mud and held fast. Harm pushed with all his might, but couldn't free it.

Howard moaned pitifully, and Harm nearly collapsed in frustration. He paused to catch his breath and gather his thoughts. There had to be a way. He lifted Howard out of the cart and laid him down beside the creek, then returned to the cart and tried to free it from the mud.

It was stuck fast. Harm went back to Howard and gave him water from his canteen.

Howard opened his eyes and fastened them on Harm. "I'm not afraid to die."

"Don't talk that way," said Harm. "We'll get you back to camp. Our surgeons will help you."

"I thought I would be. But what the *dominie* says is true. Jesus won't leave us." He closed his eyes and lost consciousness again.

The musket fire down by the river had ceased. Kees would be waiting for him at the chestnut tree. Harm went back to the hand cart and tried again to free it. But his feet kept slipping in the mud so that he couldn't get any leverage. The cart refused to budge.

A twig snapped, and Harm jumped for his musket.

"Hold your fire, soldier," said Kees. "How's our patient?"

"Not so good," said Harm. "He needs to get back to camp, but the cart is stuck."

Kees took off his coat. "Let me help." With Harm pushing and Kees pulling, they managed to free the cart and push it up the bank. Then, they went back for Howard and returned him to the cart.

Moving Howard proved easier with Kees' help. Together,

they lifted the cart over rocks and other obstructions. Soon, they reached the smooth flat road and turned back toward Kingston.

The clouds parted briefly, revealing a full moon, then enclosed it again in darkness. Keeping to the road would be risky, but taking to the woods again was out of the question.

"Any trouble at the hospital?" asked Kees.

Harm told how the surgeon had helped him, then asked, "How about you? Did you run into trouble?"

Kees grinned. "I played the wounded bird—crashed around holding my arm like I was injured. They fell for it."

He continued relaying his part in the rescue as they made their way up the pike. The night grew long, and stars disappeared from the eastern sky.

Suddenly, Kees stopped talking, then came to a halt. "Shhh. Listen."

Harm heard it, too. A wagon creaking up the pike behind them.

"We have to get off this road," said Kees.

Harm eyed the ditch on either side of the road, doubtful they could manage it with the cart.

"Take Howard," said Kees. "I'll hide the cart."

Harm managed to get both arms under Howard and lifted him out of the cart. Howard moaned, but didn't wake up. Harm slid down the ditch, then scrambled up the other side into the trees.

A covered wagon drawn by four mules rolled up, grinding to a stop just past the place where Harm and Howard lay hidden. A grizzled old man stepped down from the wagon and peered into the darkness.

Howard moaned and Harm clamped a hand over his mouth.

"Who's out there?" demanded the old man.

Harm said nothing. He wished he knew where Kees was.

The man took a step forward, then another. "I say, who's out there?"

Harm was about to answer when Kees burst from the trees, pinning the man against his wagon. He put a hand to the man's neck. "We don't want to hurt you, but we need to commandeer this wagon."

When the old man regained his composure, he looked Kees in the eye. "My name is Jericho Johnston," he said. "This wagon belongs to my employer, Mr. Staples. If you were from around here, you'd know that name. This wagon will be doing his business."

Howard moaned again, and Jericho peered into the forest. His face softened. "You've got an injured boy out there."

Harm, carrying Howard, emerged from the trees. Jericho grimaced at the sight.

"We need to get him to Kingston," said Harm.

"Kingston's where I'm bound."

"Not anymore," said Kees. "You can have your wagon back when we're done with it."

Jericho chuckled. "Our boys patrol this road. They might be curious when they find Mr. Staples' wagon being driven by two Yankees."

Kees bit his lip.

"Hide yourselves in the back," continued Jericho. "I'll get you back to your camp."

"How do we know you won't turn us over to your soldiers?" said Kees.

"We'll just have to trust each other. This boy's hurt. Let's get him where he can be helped."

Kees didn't like it, but they had no choice.

Jericho climbed up onto the box and took up the traces. "Get yourselves well-hid back there. And keep your friend quiet."

Harm lifted Howard into the back of the wagon. Kees threw a blanket over them and then hid himself.

Jericho spoke to the mules, and the wagon lurched forward. They made good time, much faster than they could have made pushing the hand cart.

"We've got to be close now," hissed Kees, just loud enough for Harm to hear.

Suddenly, a clatter of horses' hooves approached them on the road. Voices rang out, and the wagon ground to a halt.

Harm put a hand over Howard's mouth and gripped his musket with the other. He didn't dare raise his head to see what was happening outside.

The voices continued. They were Confederate soldiers, wanting to know what Jericho had in his wagon.

He assured them it was only building supplies from Louden. Mr. Staples was planning an addition to one of his barns. He expected the supplies by daylight. He was not a patient man.

The name of Mr. Staples seemed to carry weight with the rebels. Their tone changed immediately. Jericho offered them a bottle to pass among themselves. That sealed their cooperation. Soon, the sound of hooves clattered away into the distance.

Jericho's mules brayed, and the wagon pulled forward again. Harm poked his head out from under his blanket, but Jericho warned him back with a growl and a wave of his hand.

Fifteen minutes later, the wagon stopped once more. This time, Jericho called the boys up. Harm stood and stretched his legs. He smelled woodsmoke and saw a line of tents. Relief flowed over him as he saw the familiar stars and stripes.

The guards at the gate stopped the wagon. Colonel Mott emerged from his tent and approached them. He ordered Jericho down from his wagon.

Kees explained about Howard, and medical staff were called for. They whisked Howard away to the hospital.

Colonel Mott ordered Jericho held for further questioning.

"You can't," said Kees. "He helped us."

The colonel turned to Kees, demanding a reason for his absence from camp.

Kees dove into the details of Howard's rescue, his eyes bright with excitement.

Colonel Mott eyed him coolly throughout. When Kees stopped for breath, the colonel motioned to his major, "Put him in the stockade."

The major signaled to the guards.

"Wait . . ." stammered Kees, as they grabbed his arms and escorted him from the room. "You don't understand. It was a rescue . . . It was . . ."

Colonel Mott turned Harm over to Captain de Boe and returned to his tent.

"What will they do to Kees?" asked Harm.

"I wish I knew," said the captain. "Get some sleep."

Harm hadn't slept in twenty-four hours, but he wanted to be at his friend's side when he regained consciousness, so he went to the hospital instead.

"How is he?" Harm asked the surgeon.

"Not good."

Howard sensed their presence and began to thrash about. He tried to sit up. "Mother?"

The surgeon laid him back down. As Harm took his hand, Howard opened his eyes, then closed them again. "I hear singing . . ."

Harm fought back tears. Howard's body relaxed, and he drifted into unconsciousness again.

Exhaustion threatened to overcome Harm. His eyes wouldn't

stay open. He could barely stand on his feet. The surgeon suggested he get some rest, and Harm didn't argue. He returned to his tent and collapsed.

When he awoke, the sun was high overhead. He returned to the hospital.

The surgeon met him at the door. "I'm sorry. He died maybe twenty minutes ago."

Harm felt empty and cold. The bugle called his regiment to afternoon drill, but Harm ignored it. He climbed a bank and sat high above the Clinch River. The sky shimmered overhead, as blue as Lake Michigan in May. Autumn leaves fluttered in the breeze like it was any other day. A pair of gray squirrels chased each other from branch to branch as if nothing had changed.

The old questions returned. How could this be God's will?

Later, Kees climbed the bank and joined him. "I thought I might find you here."

Harm wiped at his eyes with the back of his hand. "You break out of the stockade?"

"Captain de Boe put in a good word for me."

"What about Jericho?"

"They questioned him and let him go."

"Good."

Kees tossed a rock into the river. "You think we did the right thing bringing Howard here?"

Harm nodded. "Our surgeon told me he'd have died either way. And he belongs here. His friends are here."

Later, back at the tents, Harm wrote a letter to inform Howard's family of his death. He struggled to find the right words. In the end, he left out most of the details, but told them Howard had returned to his company before he died. At the very last, he'd spoken of his faith and his family. He would receive a proper burial with Scripture and the prayers of his friends.

The 25th Michigan remained in Kingston throughout November, while the rebels remained in Louden. Two weeks passed before the bugle announced mail call. Harm received three letters. The first was from his brother, Sam, who told Harm not to believe everything Rinze said about him. He intended to stay on the farm unless his name came up in the draft. Or, if Henry's name came up, he'd offer himself as a substitute. Henry had Anna and now Eliza to care for.

The second letter was from his parents. They informed him that all Holland grieved the loss of Howard. Rev. van Raalte became so choked up in his congregational prayer he couldn't continue for a long moment. The Tillema family continued strong in faith, but Sarah wept through the entire worship service and wasn't able to attend in the evening.

The third letter was from the Tillemas themselves. It consisted of just a few lines.

---

*Thank you for your letter regarding our dear son, Howard. We are sorely grieved at his passing but comforted to know that he died among friends. Jesus said, "I am the resurrection, and the life: he that believeth in me, though he were dead, yet shall he live" (John 11:25).*

---

Harm turned the letter over to make sure. There was nothing from Sarah.

## CHAPTER 30

# DECEMBER 1863 – APRIL 1864

As the weather turned colder, the great armies of the East settled into winter quarters on either side of the Rappahannock River. In Tennessee, the 25th Michigan left Kingston and moved to the banks of the Holston River near Strawberry Plains.

Harm hated to leave the place where they'd buried Howard. Three weeks later, they moved again. Each time they moved camp, Harm felt he was leaving Howard further behind.

On Christmas Eve, the regiment camped near Mossy Creek. Harm and his friends gathered for devotions. Ted read the Christmas story from Matthew 1, focusing on verse 21: *"And she shall bring forth a son, and thou shalt call his name JESUS: for he shall save his people from their sins."*

"I wish I could read Hebrew and Greek," said Gerrit. "Lots of names in the Bible mean things in the original languages."

"But this verse tells us what the name Jesus means," said Kees.

Gerrit nodded. "It's an important name, too. It tells us why he came—to save us from our sins."

"Isn't that obvious?" asked Ted.

"It should be. But we don't like to admit we need saving. My

39

father's minister back in the Netherlands denied Jesus was even the Son of God."

"The Bible calls him the Son of God."

"The Son of God and the Son of man," said Gerrit. "Both are true. The name Emmanuel combines both ideas—God with us."

"God with us," said Ted. "That's Christmas in a nutshell."

"Then there's Messiah and Christ," said Gerrit. "They both mean Anointed One. One is Hebrew, the other Greek."

"I thought you didn't know Hebrew and Greek."

Gerrit turned red. "I guess I know that much."

Kees scratched his chin. "You can tell how important Jesus is just by the number of names and titles the Bible gives him. There must be a hundred."

They all joined in, listing as many as they could think of.

"Lamb of God."

"Bread of Life."

"Light of the World."

"Good Shepherd."

"Savior."

"Alpha and Omega."

"King of kings and Lord of lords."

"The Last Adam."

"The Image of the invisible God."

"The Way, the Truth, and the Life."

"The one Mediator between God and men."

When the names and titles stopped coming, talk died down. After a bit, Gerrit said, "This is our second Christmas away from home."

"Feeling homesick?" asked Kees.

"I'm not ashamed to admit it. Hearing Arend and Rinze talk about home made me realize how much I miss it. Losing Howard made it worse. I've almost forgotten what church is like."

"It's been too long," agreed Kees. "Lebanon, wasn't it? Or Munfordville. I can't remember."

"Lebanon," said Ted. "That red-faced minister."

"Right. I remember Gerrit didn't like him much."

Gerrit shot him a look. "None of us did. Remember? He just kept saying, 'God is love. God is love.'"

Kees grinned. "God *is* love."

"But he's righteous and holy, too. You can't just take one thing and ignore everything else. God doesn't wink at sin."

Ted nodded. "That's what Christmas is all about. He sent Jesus to save us from sin."

"Good tidings of great joy," said Kees.

"It's easy to forget, though," said Gerrit. "Especially when we're not in church every Sunday. It makes me wonder sometimes if we made the right decision."

Kees looked at him. "What are you saying? We shouldn't have come?"

"I'm just saying . . . I wonder sometimes."

Kees hooted. "Gerrit breaks with Rev. van Raalte. The civil war comes home."

Harm enjoyed devotions with his friends, but his joy in the season was dimmed by thoughts of Sarah and the rest of the Tillema family who must face the holiday without their brother and son.

A couple of days later, scouts reported rebel activity in a nearby town called Dandridge. A detachment was sent south to investigate, but the 25th Michigan remained at Mossy Creek.

Later that morning, the clatter of musket fire sounded from the outer pickets. The drums played the long roll, and the bugle called the alarm.

"Form up," ordered Captain de Boe.

Harm grabbed his musket from the stacked arms outside his tent and took his place with the rest of the company.

"Rebels are advancing from Talbott's Station," said the captain. "It seems Dandridge was a diversion." He ordered Harm and his friends to take up defensive positions.

Harm dug in behind a pile of fallen logs and prepared for the rebels to arrive. All morning, the sound of musket fire drew nearer. He'd eaten a big breakfast, and it settled like a rock in his belly.

Finally, he caught sight of the rebels off to his left. The two lines traded fire. The rebels focused their artillery fire on the area to Harm's left, an area held by the 118th Ohio.

The bombardment was withering, forcing the 118th Ohio to fall back. Captain de Boe ordered his company to fall back with them.

"We can hold them off," said Kees.

The captain shook his head. "The 118th Ohio can't. We have to protect their flank."

All afternoon, the rebels advanced on Harm's left, pushing the 118th Ohio back. The 25th Michigan fell back as well, in order to cover their flank.

By late afternoon, the Union soldiers were backed up against Mossy Creek.

Then, suddenly, a fresh cannonade filled the air.

"Who is that?" Kees stood up to get a better look, then sunk down again as musket balls buzzed all about him.

"They're ours," said Gerrit. "Look!"

It was true. The rebels were under attack. Clouds of dust and debris filled the wood as Union artillery pounded their position. The 118th Ohio left their defensive works and pushed forward toward the confused rebels.

Captain de Boe ordered his troops to advance as well. Harm

scrambled forward and fired into the rebels. After a morning spent in retreat, it felt good to advance. The rebels fell back the way they'd come, retreating toward Talbott's Station. Harm and his friends pursued them until dusk, then made their way back to camp.

The 25th Michigan had received only minor injuries, but the 118th Ohio had taken heavy casualties, forty injured and two killed.

"Who was that at the end?" asked Kees. "They sure turned the tide."

"Our own detachment," said Willem. "Somehow they got word and returned from Dandridge."

Kees whistled. "Just in time."

After the battle at Mossy Creek, the weather turned bitter cold and both armies settled in for the winter. Ice formed on the river. Some still went without boots. Harm and his friends placed logs in a stockade pattern at the base of their tents and chinked them with mud to insulate them.

February passed quietly as they remained in winter quarters, conserving their warmth, strength, and supplies. Kees got his hands on a length of stove pipe which allowed them to build a fire inside their tent and vent the smoke outside. Long days with little to do were a welcome relief, but Harm continued to grieve the loss of Howard.

March brought warmer weather. Union forces advanced on all fronts. Confederate forces withdrew from Knoxville and retreated into the rugged country of Northern Georgia.

Once, Harm and his friends stumbled on one of their abandoned camps. It was full of blackened railroad cars and artillery carts. Some were charred and smoking. Others had been backed into the river.

"They must have left in a hurry," said Willem. "They couldn't get their heavy equipment out so they left it behind."

Kees agreed. "They didn't want us to use this stuff, so they destroyed it."

With the rebels gone, the 25th Michigan camped outside Knoxville, waiting for the next big campaign. At mail call, Harm received a letter from Sarah.

---

*Holland, Michigan*
*March 5, 1864*

*Dear Harm,*

*I'm sorry I haven't written sooner. We still grieve the loss of my dear brother, Howard. But I want you to know that we are all comforted by the fact that he died among friends.*

*We miss him every day, but we submit to God's will and would not wish him back. He has entered his final rest and awaits us in glory.*

*My mother spoke recently with your Aunt Nel who heard from Willem of your daring rescue. I cannot express the depths of my gratitude and admiration for your noble effort.*

*As hard as it is to know that Howard will not return, we are thankful he did not have to endure one of those awful prison camps. Also, your witness to his faithfulness is of great comfort to us all.*

*Once again, I thank you for your bravery. And now I ask you to refrain from further actions which would put you in danger, as I most earnestly await the day of your return.*

*My prayer continues that God will keep you safe and return you to me.*

*Sarah*

Harm carried the letter in his coat pocket and read it numerous times each day as the weather turned warm and spring burst out all around him. He wrote Sarah a reply, but he had no desire to write about the fighting. Instead, he filled the pages with the beauty that surrounded him. He wrote of boulder-strewn streams, flowering dogwoods, and indigo buntings flitting from branch to branch. He closed by thanking Sarah for her letter and telling her he looked forward to the day they'd be reunited.

Later, Willem suggested they visit Spencer and Clay, as they did from time to time. They found Spencer in front of his tent, playing a violin with some of the other regimental musicians.

Spencer grinned when he saw them coming, and held up the violin. "I bought it off a cavalry officer. No idea where he got it. He couldn't play a note."

Harm admired the instrument. The wood was stained a deep reddish-brown, bringing out its natural beauty. It was carved and curved into an intricate design.

"It's made of spruce and maple," said Spencer. "The strings are catgut."

"Catgut?"

"I know. It comes from sheep's intestines, not cats. The bow is made with horsehair."

"Let's hear how it sounds."

One of the musicians, a man in his fifties with a close-cropped goatee, began to strum a guitar. Spencer tucked the violin under his chin, drew the bow across the strings and fingered the notes with his left hand.

The resulting music left Harm entranced. He marveled at the

violin's ability to bring out the emotion in a tune. When Spencer finished, Harm said, "I love it."

Spencer smiled. "I knew you would."

"Was that Beethoven?"

Spencer chuckled. "He *did* write some beautiful music for violin, but it's too difficult for me."

"So, what was that?"

"'Gentle Annie,' by Stephen Foster."

"Did he write any others?"

"Lots." He played another Stephen Foster tune, "Nelly was a Lady."

Again, Harm was amazed. How could horsehair dragged across catgut strung to a wooden frame produce sounds that rivaled the human voice for beauty?

When Spencer finished, Willem said, "One more."

Harm agreed. "Do you know any psalms?"

"Sorry, I don't. But you might know this one."

The tune began softly and slowly, then built steadily into a stirring anthem. Harm hardly drew a breath as Spencer played. He didn't recognize the tune, but wanted to know more.

"It's "A Mighty Fortress is Our God,'" said Spencer.

"Bach?" ventured Harm.

"Luther."

"*Martin* Luther?"

"It's true. He wrote lots of hymns."

"How about John Calvin? Did he write any hymns?"

"Not that I know of. But he may have put some psalms into verse for singing."

Harm was impressed the Reformers took time to provide songs for worship. He was also impressed with Spencer's knowledge. "Where did you learn that?"

"At home. My folks love music."

Harm remembered the last time Spencer had spoken of his parents. "You said before that they are hypocrites."

"They are. They can be so frustrating, the way they say one thing and do another."

Willem nodded. "That's pretty much the definition of a hypocrite."

"It is," said Harm. "But none of us live up to our principles all the time. That doesn't make us hypocrites, necessarily. Just weak."

Spencer groaned. "Don't take that away from me, Harm. That's how I stay angry at them."

Harm's visits with Spencer came to an end as April brought renewed activity to the camp. With re-established supply lines, the army busied itself distributing food and clothing to all. Those who'd been laid low with sickness recovered and returned to service. New troops arrived, and the size of the army swelled. The 25th Michigan resumed drill by company, regiment, and brigade.

Gerrit frowned. "It feels like the war is starting up again."

"General Sherman is planning a campaign to take Atlanta," said Willem. "It's the biggest manufacturing center left in the South."

"How far is that from here?" asked Kees.

"Two hundred miles."

"No problem. We've done that before."

"One problem," offered Ted, "sixty thousand rebels waiting to welcome us to Georgia."

General Henry Judah, commander of the Division that included the 25th Michigan, issued extra uniforms to all his soldiers whether they needed them or not. He deducted the cost from their pay. No one cared much for General Judah.

"All that extra weight on a two-hundred-mile march," said Kees. "It's foolish."

"It's a crime," said Gerrit.

"It's an order," said Ted.

"It's almost summer," said Kees. "He's mad."

"He's a thief," said Gerrit.

"He's a general," said Ted.

For the Atlanta campaign, General Sherman gathered three large armies. The Army of the Cumberland, the Army of the Tennessee, and the Army of the Ohio—which included the 25th Michigan—formed a fighting force of some 100,000 soldiers. At the same time, in the east, General Grant and the Army of the Potomac prepared to advance on Richmond.

The first week of May, the armies set out for Atlanta. Summer came early and with it, unbearable heat. Harm and his friends stopped at every creek to fill their canteens. Kees made a habit of stripping off his shirt, dipping it in the creek, and wringing the water over his head.

By noon, soldiers began to rid themselves of their extra coats. Smoke trailed behind them as piles of cast-off uniforms were burned.

Kees bemoaned a lost business opportunity. "If I had a wagon, I'd gather them up and resell them to the U.S. Government."

"General Judah would just resell them to us," said Ted.

A couple days into the march, they came to a halt in the town of Red Clay. Harm took advantage of the break to sketch a supply train as it crossed over a trestle bridge outside of town.

The next day, they entered Georgia, leaving much of their supply line behind them. General Sherman expected them to live off the land. The quartermaster procured what food he could, but farmers in Northern Georgia had no intention of helping the Union Army.

Soldiers were expected to fend for themselves with private foraging raids. Many abused the policy, taking not only food but anything they wanted. They returned to camp with stolen blankets and tools, even bank notes and jewelry.

Harm and his friends discussed it at devotions. "We don't have a choice," said Kees. "It's forage or starve."

Gerrit disagreed. "We should obey God rather than men."

"We can't disobey orders, though," insisted Willem.

"Daniel refused to obey the king's command."

"Israel kept the spoils when they fought other nations," argued Kees. "That's part of war."

Willem agreed. "It's only bacon and beans. I've seen soldiers do a lot worse."

Harm felt torn. He didn't want to forage, but to disobey orders meant the stockade for sure and possibly starvation.

"General Sherman expects it," said Willem. "It's part of his war strategy."

Right or wrong, the justification of official sanction from General Sherman broke down their resistance. But they agreed to take only what they needed to survive.

Soon enough, Harm and his friends found themselves on the doorstep of a tidy Georgia farmhouse. Kees knocked on the door. No one answered. He knocked again.

The door creaked open, and an old man appeared. He leaned against the door frame, as thin as air. He spoke with an accent so thick they couldn't make out what he said.

"We need food," said Kees, motioning to his mouth like the man was deaf.

An old woman appeared in the doorway. "Go away." She nearly spit out the words as she slammed the door closed.

Harm was ready to walk away but Kees simply moved to the

barn. He posted Ted in the yard to make sure the old couple didn't try something foolish, and directed Harm to search a pile of hay that filled one corner of the barn.

Harm grabbed a pitchfork and began to make his way through the pile.

"This is a waste of time," said Gerrit. "You saw how thin they were. They're starving."

Kees dismissed that with a wave of his hand. "Keep looking."

Halfway through the stack Harm discovered something. He scraped away more hay, revealing a stash of salt pork and a barrel of cider.

"Starving, eh?" said Kees. "Everybody, take what you can carry. I'll roll the barrel back to camp."

"We don't need this much," said Harm. "Why take more than we need?"

Kees considered that. "No. You're right. We'd just have to carry the extra on our backs."

He settled on a quarter of the pork, and they each filled their canteens with cider. Harm felt good about leaving the old couple most of their provisions. But as they left the barn, the old woman appeared in the doorway again. She pointed a boney finger at them, screeching. "Thieves! Stinking, rotten, thieving, Yankee dogs!"

Back at camp, Kees laughed about the old woman. But Harm couldn't help seeing things from her point of view. His mother would do the same thing if someone tried to steal one of her chickens.

"I agree we shouldn't take more than we need," said Willem. "But we can't allow ourselves to get undernourished either. Any day now, we'll be in the biggest battle of our lives."

As much as Harm hated foraging, it became almost routine.

The farmers all claimed to have no food. But Kees always managed to find some hidden away in the corner of a barn, the back of a wood lot, or the bottom of a well. Harm learned to ignore the farmers' pitiful looks and tune out their curses. But his prayers suffered, as he found it hard to say "Give us this day our daily bread" when it had been taken under threat of force.

A week into their march on Atlanta, Harm received a letter from his family. They were thankful for his safety and good health, and prayed God would continue to protect him. The weather back home was cool and dry. Father and Sam were busy in the fields. Little Eliza, now seventeen months, was walking and talking. She could say Mama and Papa, and Oma and Opa. They were teaching her to say "Harm," but it mostly came out as "Ahm."

Harm was thrilled to receive news from home, but his heart sank when he saw a slip of paper in the bottom of the envelope, written in his father's hand.

———

*Harm,*

*I'm afraid Ted's father has only gotten worse since I last wrote. At this time, he is given to public drunkenness and disorderly conduct. I inform you in hopes you can help Ted deal with this news as it becomes known in your company.*

*Love, Father*

———

Ted was down by the creek doing his laundry. Seeing Harm coming, he asked, "Why the long face?"

"I got another note from my father."

Ted stood up. "Should I brace myself?" He read the note and

handed it back to Harm. "It's all right. I've seen it before. He's just not hiding it anymore."

"You want to talk about it?"

Ted shook his head. "Honestly, Harm, I don't think you could understand." He returned to his laundry, keeping his face turned away from Harm.

Harm felt he should say something more but what? He put a hand on Ted's shoulder, then returned to the tents.

The next day, they resumed their march. They followed the Tennessee and Atlantic rail line south. General Johnston and the Confederate Army of Tennessee had dug in at a place called Dalton. The city was guarded from the north by Rocky Face Ridge, a ribbon of rock which jutted up six hundred feet above the surrounding countryside.

The 25th Michigan approached a portion of the ridge called Buzzard Roost. Captain de Boe gave the order to advance. Ted didn't wait for the others. He charged ahead.

Harm watched him, puzzled. Ted never shirked his duty but he rarely led an advance. What was he up to?

Sixty feet up the ridge, they came under fire. Rebels, positioned higher up, rained down artillery and musket fire on them.

Harm scrambled for shelter, sweat dripping down his forehead and stinging his eyes. He hunkered down behind the protection of a large boulder. Ted braced himself between two rocks but continued to fire up the ridge, ignoring deadly volleys of rebel musketry.

Harm watched in disbelief. What was Ted thinking? Did he hope to get injured so he could return home? Or be killed so he wouldn't have to?

Captain de Boe called up Union artillery to support them. The big guns pounded the ridge above them. Eventually, rebels abandoned their positions and retreated higher up the ridge. The 25th Michigan pursued. Again, Ted led the charge.

Sixty feet further they came under fire again. Harm sought cover behind a pile of fallen timbers. Ted ducked behind a tree, but continued to fire up the ridge.

Union artillery followed behind and pounded the rebels once again. Sixty feet at a time, they pushed higher up the ridge. Each assault brought new casualties. Each break in the cannonade revealed the cries of wounded soldiers.

Then, suddenly, Captain de Boe received orders to call off the assault.

"We're so close," said Ted. "We can take the summit."

"Fall back."

Back in camp, the captain tried to explain. "They have the advantage in this terrain, just like we did at Tebbs Bend."

"So, we just give up?" asked Ted.

"We don't need it. Tomorrow, we'll march south, get around their flank, and move on. It's Atlanta we're after."

Later that night, the postmaster put out word that mail would go out the next morning. Everyone busied themselves with letters home. Harm urged his family not to fear, despite his own sense of foreboding that the march on Atlanta would come at great cost.

## CHAPTER 31

# MAY 1864

A cool spring helped the tulips thrive along the paths outside the van Wyke home. Mother and Trina sat on the front step, enjoying the soft light of morning. The tulips seemed to glow from some inner light—yellow as the goldfinches, orange as the orioles.

At noon, Father took a break from the fields and returned to the house for a hearty dinner. Father offered thanks for the food that God had graciously provided. He asked God's blessing on the family's labors, whether it be in the fields, the home, or school. He asked God to guard and protect Harm and the rest of his company.

Later, Father went to town and was rewarded with a letter from Harm. The family gathered that evening, and Father read.

———

Dalton, Georgia
May 13, 1864
Dear Father, Mother, and family at home,

"Cannons to right of us, cannons to left of us, cannons in front of us, volleyed and thundered!" We have seen heavy fighting on Rocky Face Ridge outside Dalton. We were ordered to take the towering ridge of rock and timber. The rebels who held it strongly objected. After many a shot and shell, someone had the bright idea to go around the ridge. I would they had thought of that earlier.

By God's grace I came through it well and am as strong as ever. My prayer is that you also enjoy good health.

We will likely face more battles as we move toward Atlanta. But don't fear. The Lord will watch over us here in Georgia just as he watches over you in Holland.

---

Father stopped reading. No one spoke for a long time.

Then Sam said, "They're into it now."

Father nodded. "It seems."

"Why do they call it Rocky Face Ridge?" asked Trina.

Father didn't know.

Sam thought maybe it was one of those outcroppings where, if you look at it just right, you can see a face in the rock.

"Maybe," agreed Father. He turned back to the letter.

---

We have had to forage if we want to eat. It's not so easy nor so pleasant. I'll try to explain when I return.

---

"What's 'forage?'" asked Trina.

"The army doesn't always have enough food," said Sam. "Soldiers have to find food along the way."

"Where do they find it?"

Sam glanced at Mother and continued carefully. "I suppose they could catch fish. Pick berries, maybe."

Mother, thank you for your letter dated May 1, which I received on the 10th. Thank you also for sending me a copy of *De Hollander* newspaper. News from home is always welcome.

Father, the latest regarding Mr. Vogel is very sad. It is hard on Ted, as you can imagine. Please keep him in your prayers.

Sam, I've enclosed a drawing of a train crossing over a trestle bridge. These sometimes stretch hundreds of feet over rivers and streams. You would think they are too rickety to support a wagon, much less a locomotive.

Father held up the drawing of the railroad trestle for all to see.

"Can we go on a railroad?" asked Trina.

"We don't have a railroad in Holland," said Father.

"Not yet," said Sam. "There's talk of adding a line from Kalamazoo soon. Grand Rapids, too."

"Where would you like to go on the railroad?" asked Mother.

Trina considered. "Rocky Face Ridge."

Mother smiled. "So, you can see Harm?"

"Yes, but . . . I want to see that face in the rock, too."

Father smiled and turned back to the letter.

Georgia feels much different than Tennessee. For one thing, the earth is covered in thick red clay. I'd love to learn more about it. I think it is not good for farming. But there is a pine tree here with a very interesting cone. It stays tightly closed, sometimes for many years. But that's good. If its seeds fell to the ground the tall trees would block out the sun and they wouldn't grow. But when

a fire sweeps through the forest and clears out the tall trees, the cones sense the heat and immediately open up. In this way God watches over even the trees of the forest.

I pray you will remain healthy and enjoy a good growing season. As for us, we await God's will.

Your loving son and brother, Harm VanWyke

Mother placed the letter in a corner of the cupboard along with Harm's other letters. Sam helped Trina hang the drawing of the train on the wall.

Later, Father and Mother sat alone on the front porch, watching a doe and two speckled fawns moving across the lane.

"Will there be more fighting?" she asked.

He sighed. "The South won't give up Atlanta without a fight. It's too important to them."

"That's what I thought." Then she brightened. "That was a very nice drawing. He's quite talented."

He nodded.

She said, "Jacob saw it. He always encouraged Harm."

"I . . ." His voice caught in his throat. "I wish . . ."

She looked at him. "What?"

"It would have been nice if . . . if his own father had encouraged him."

She laid her head on his shoulder. "One thing Harm has never lacked is a father's love."

## CHAPTER 32

# MAY – JULY 1864

The morning after their assault on Rocky Face Ridge, the 25th Michigan marched fifteen miles south and slipped east through a gap in the ridge. Harm tried several times to ask Ted about his charge up the hill, but Ted carefully avoided his questions. They emerged south of Dalton above the city of Resaca. Meanwhile, the rebels had pulled back from Dalton and re-established their lines in front of Resaca.

Approaching Resaca, their company emerged from the woods and came to a halt at the edge of a broad meadow. Kees pointed to elaborately constructed defensive works at the far edge of the meadow.

"Maybe they're empty," said Gerrit, hopefully.

Captain de Boe ordered an advance, and the Union soldiers left the protection of the trees. Crickets skittered and buzzed at each step. The late afternoon sun turned everything golden. Water rippled in some unseen creek.

Harm was nearly halfway across the meadow when the afternoon erupted in musket fire. Puffs of smoke rose from the rebel works, and musket balls sliced through the air.

"Let's go," cried Kees. He and Ted charged forward together.

Harm hesitated. A soldier to his left fell, clutching his side. Somewhere behind him, another cried out.

After a moment of indecision, Harm followed Kees and Ted, along with several dozen others. An equal number scrambled back to the safety of the trees.

Kees outpaced Ted and soon led him by a dozen yards. From the rebel works came a sharp rattle of musket fire. Kees fell and disappeared in the tall grass.

Ted pulled up. "He's down! Kees went down!"

Harm joined Ted a hundred yards from the rebel works. "We can't stay here." Together, they raced on.

The muskets fired again. More soldiers fell.

Harm searched the ground as he ran. Where was Kees?

Suddenly, the ground fell away in front of him and he stumbled forward. He felt himself falling and cried out in alarm. A creek, hidden from sight, wound across the meadow. Harm spilled over the bank and into the water. He rose up sputtering for breath, only to be driven back down as Ted landed on top of him.

Someone reached out a hand and helped Harm to his feet. It was Kees, spattered with mud but unhurt. "You all right?" asked Kees. They stood in a foot of water, protected from the rebels by a high bank.

As soon as Kees was convinced that Harm and Ted were all right, he splashed down the creek, looking for others who'd made it that far. When he returned, he was followed by Gerrit and two dozen others.

"What now?" asked Gerrit.

"Now, we finish what we started." Kees scrambled up the bank. Rebel muskets responded immediately, and a ball struck the bank just inches from his face. He slid back down.

"Finished so soon?" asked Ted.

Kees grinned. "That'll do for now."

"We have to get back," said a boy named Nelson. "If they send out skirmishers, we're finished."

"Our company is still up there," said Kees. "The rebels won't dare leave their little fortress."

Nelson looked unconvinced. "So we just sit here, like ducks on a pond?"

Ted tossed a stick into the water. "Ducks seem to enjoy it."

Nelson paced back and forth nervously, then, without warning, scrambled up the bank and raced back across the field. Muskets rang out from the rebel works. Then, silence. Kees sprang up the bank to see what had happened, but immediately drew fire and slid back down.

"Did he make it? Do you think he made it?" asked Gerrit.

Kees didn't respond.

They spent the rest of the day clinging to the bank, their legs half in the water, waiting for evening to fall.

Harm took the opportunity to talk with Ted. "You led the charge at Rocky Face Ridge. Now, this. You trying to be a hero or something?"

Ted shrugged. "I thought I'd give it a try, yeah."

"Why?"

He didn't answer immediately. Harm waited. They weren't going anywhere.

After several minutes, Ted said, "I thought maybe if I came out of this war a hero, I'd be able to show my face back home."

"You don't have to do that."

"It would be a lot easier, though, if the headlines read, 'General Sherman couldn't have done it without Ted Vogel.'"

"You don't need that. Gerrit will be a minister. Willem will probably be the mayor. They'll stand up for you."

"And you?"

"Me? Of course. But Kees will be a captain of industry. The leading citizens will all be at your side."

Ted didn't respond for a long time, then said, "And my getting killed would ruin all that?"

"Exactly."

"Thanks, Harm."

"So, no more playing the hero?"

Ted smiled. "Truth is, I didn't much care for it."

Dusk came, and shadows crept across the field. Kees put his cap on a willow branch and raised it into the air. It brought no response from the rebels. "This is our chance. Stay low. Don't bunch up."

One by one they clambered up the bank and crept back toward the tree line. Halfway back, Ted hissed, "Harm, help me."

Harm angled in Ted's direction. "What's wrong?"

"I found Nelson."

The boy lay motionless at Ted's feet, but he revived when Harm touched his arm. "I'm hit," he said. "I can't feel my leg."

Harm and Ted each took a shoulder and dragged him toward the trees. They were almost there when Nelson's foot caught on a rock and he cried out in pain. Rebel muskets flashed in the darkness. Musket balls smacked the ground all around. Harm lost his grip and fell backwards.

"Don't leave me," pleaded Nelson.

Ted hunched beside him. "We're not going anywhere."

Grabbing his shoulders again, they pulled him to the safety of the trees. Stretcher bearers were waiting to carry him to the regimental hospital.

Harm and Ted returned to the tents. Five members of Company I had been injured. Cornelius van Dam, just one year older than Harm and well-liked by all, had been killed.

"They know they can't win," fumed Kees. "But still they fight. They're like animals."

"Worse," said Willem. "Devils."

"Get some sleep," advised Captain de Boe. "We'll face them again tomorrow."

The next morning, the 25th Michigan returned to the meadow. This time they approached the rebel works through the trees that bordered the meadow on the left. By mid-morning, they were in position to attack along the rebels' right flank. Captain de Boe gave the order to "fix bayonets."

Harm's hand trembled as he fixed his bayonet. Nelson's blood still darkened the sleeve of his coat.

They left the cover of the trees and advanced on the rebel works. Harm expected the morning to erupt, but all remained quiet. Finally, at twenty yards out, Kees charged. He covered the last twenty yards at full speed and leapt over the works with his bayonet poised for close combat.

Harm scrambled behind, expecting a bloody battle. But the rebels were gone. They'd abandoned their position in the night.

The same story repeated itself all over Resaca. The rebels had fled.

"This war is over," said Kees. "Atlanta is ours."

"How surprised they'll be," said Ted.

"It's true, though. They couldn't stop us at Dalton, even with Rocky Face Ridge. They couldn't hold us here, even dug in behind defensive works. What hope do they have of stopping us anywhere else?"

The advance on Atlanta continued in good spirits. Confident of his superior numbers, General Sherman split his forces. The Army of the Cumberland followed the rail line south to Cassville, driving the Confederate Army back toward Atlanta, while the

Army of the Ohio, including the 25th Michigan, swung south first, then east toward Cassville.

By the time Harm and his friends could see the town in the distance, the rebels had all been swept out of the area. For the first time in weeks, they marched without fear of opposition. The sun shimmered in a cloudless sky. Indigo buntings flitted about in the trees.

When they reached the main street, however, the mood changed. The Army of the Cumberland had loosed their vengeance on Cassville. Buildings had been reduced to piles of smoking rubble. Walls of houses had been pulled down, exposing parlors and bedrooms. A grandfather clock lay toppled and charred. A portrait of a fine old couple had been pierced through with a bayonet.

"What happened here?" asked Kees.

"Us, I think," said Ted.

"Can't be," said Kees. "It's more like . . ."

"Animals?" said Ted. "Devils?"

Harm knew better. This had been done by soldiers just like himself. Was his regiment capable of this kind of destruction? Was his company? Was he?

He marched through the town in stunned silence. A young girl with matted hair sat alone on a blackened porch. An old woman teetered aimlessly down the street, her mouth moving but making no sound.

"Listen!" said Kees. What's that?"

Harm heard it, too. Piano music. He recognized one of Beethoven's melancholy tunes. He turned a corner, and the music grew louder.

"There!" Kees pointed.

When the Army of the Cumberland had taken the city, they'd

thrust a pianoforte from a fine old home's second floor to the street below. The impact had left its box cracked and its legs splayed. But Spencer had somehow worked his way to the keys and was playing the solemn tune. Clay stood beside him, keeping the beat with his drum.

That night at devotions, Ted read James 4, focusing on verse 1: *"From whence come wars and fightings among you? come they not hence, even of your lusts that war in your members?"*

They sang Psalm 119:

*O Lord, how shall a youth preserve his way,*
*At every turn by vanity surrounded?*
*In truth, if he thy statutes will obey,*
*If on thy word his attitudes are founded.*
*Thou whom I've sought, O let me never stray*
*From thy commandments, lest I be confounded.*

Kees said, "It's terrible what they did to that town. War makes people do awful things."

"It's not only war," argued Gerrit. "We're all sinful by nature."

"But people don't act like this during peacetime."

"It's there, though," Gerrit insisted. "When times are good, we learn to hide it. War exposes what's already there."

"This is no gentleman's war," said Willem. "This is what we'll face from here on out."

Harm felt it, too. They'd fought at Tebbs Bend. They'd fought numerous battles around Knoxville. But this march on Atlanta would require more of them than anything they'd seen. They would face rebel resistance at every turn.

The next morning, they continued on toward Atlanta. At Etowah River, they battled from sunup until sundown. At Kingston it was much the same. At Allatoona they battled for four days, capturing a dozen prisoners with tattered uniforms and gaunt faces.

"Why fight?" asked Kees. "You know you can't win."

"We just have to hold out," they answered. "Help is on the way."

"Help? Who?"

"England. France. They need our cotton."

That worried Harm. What would happen if the powers of Europe agreed to help the South?

The next day, they continued south, battling every step of the way. Confederate soldiers fought with fierce determination as they defended homes and land that belonged to their own families. But Union forces with superior numbers continued to outflank them, forcing them to fall back.

The advance stalled when the armies faced several days of unrelenting rain. Then the march resumed, and they entered mountainous country. They battled at Pine Mountain, and again at Lost Mountain. Each day, they advanced. Each night, they tended their wounded.

Always Harm could hear the thunder of cannons. Muskets rattled just over the nearest ridge as he ate his meals. One day, a stray ball dropped a fellow soldier as he stooped to make a pot of coffee.

Harm had a hard time sleeping. Once, he dreamed the red clay opened up beneath them and swallowed the entire company. He awoke so shaken he could hardly breathe.

At Kennesaw Mountain, they faced heavily wooded hills which made it difficult to move large numbers of soldiers. "We can't outflank them in these mountains," said Captain de Boe. "General Sherman is ordering a frontal attack."

The Union soldiers marched forward and soon came under

fire from a thousand muskets. Smoke billowed from the top of the mountain as rebels rained fire down on them.

"Where are they?" shouted Kees. "I can't see anything."

Harm fired blindly into the smoke, reloaded, advanced, and fired again. Hour after hour it continued. The rattle of musket fire was broken only by the roar of the cannons. Soldiers lay where they fell. Finally, darkness settled over the field. They'd advanced perhaps a hundred yards.

The fighting resumed the next day. And the next. Cannonballs furrowed the ground and tore the tops off trees. After three days of bloodshed, the rebels abandoned their positions and fell back once again. General Sherman ordered immediate pursuit.

By the time they reached Nickajack Creek, they'd spent forty-five days in continuous combat, though Harm had lost track of time and any sense of the world beyond the battlefield.

On the 4th of July, his friends pulled him aside. "It's Independence Day," said Kees. "Try to smile."

Harm didn't feel much like smiling.

"You should write home," said Gerrit. "Your family is probably worried about you."

It was true, his family probably *was* worried about him. He hadn't written since Cassville. But what could he write? The war was too awful.

"At least write Sarah," said Ted.

Harm bit hard to keep his emotions down. "What's the point? Who wants to read about *this*?" The truth was, he was having trouble even picturing Sarah's face.

Kees put a hand on his shoulder. "Write about something else, then. Write about your plans after the war."

"I'm not sure the war will ever end."

"Of course it will. Once Atlanta falls, we'll head home and get our hero's welcome."

Harm managed a half-smile.

Later, when it was just the two of them, Kees said, "Listen. I'm leading devotions tonight. You coming?"

Harm didn't respond. He wasn't sure he was in the mood for devotions. Kees poked a finger in his chest. "If you're not there, I'll sic Gerrit on you."

At devotions, Kees read Romans 8:28: *"And we know that all things work together for good to them that love God, to them who are the called according to his purpose."*

They sang Psalm 27:

*God is my light, my refuge, my salvation.*
*Whom shall I fear? The Lord comes to my aid.*
*He is my strength in all my tribulation.*
*Of whom shall I then ever be afraid?*
*When foes who seek my life close in on me,*
*They all shall stumble and in anguish flee;*
*And though an army should in war draw near,*
*I will be confident. I will not fear.*

They remembered their victory at Tebbs Bend on the Green River exactly one year earlier, and prayed that God would continue to watch over them in the present fighting. Despite himself, Harm felt better.

Later, Captain de Boe poked his head into their tent. "Sorry to break up your fun, but General Sherman says this is no time for a picnic. Get some sleep. In the morning, we press on."

"The 4th of July seems like a *great* time for a picnic," said Ted. "What's the hurry?"

"It's because of the election," explained Willem. "General Sherman needs to take Atlanta by November."

"What's the election have to do with it?" asked Harm.

"Everything," said Willem. "If Atlanta falls before the election, Lincoln will win in a landslide."

"And what if it doesn't fall?"

Kees grinned. "It will."

Talk of the election bothered Harm. President Lincoln seemed like a man of integrity. Would he let ambition for re-election guide his war policy?

It was dark when devotions ended, but Harm managed to scribble a few lines to Sarah. He asked how things were going at home. He asked about her family. He couldn't tell her about the war, not the real war. So, he told her about the heat and the insects. He told her he hoped the war would end soon. He read what he'd written. It wasn't much of a letter. He added a bit more.

---

I wish I could write a long letter describing the events that consume my days, but for months now it has been war, war, war. I don't have the words to describe it and would not wish for you to have to read it. So please be content in the knowledge that you are ever in my thoughts and prayers.

Harm

---

## CHAPTER 33

# JULY – OCTOBER 1864

General Sherman's combined armies reached Atlanta in late July. He didn't have enough troops to surround the city, so he focused on cutting off the major roads and rail lines. He sent the 25th Michigan and the rest of the Army of the Ohio south to take the Atlanta & West Point railroad.

Harm and his friends marched long hours in the Georgia heat, sweat stinging their eyes and soaking their uniforms. After several days, they came to a halt at Utoy Creek, just a mile from the rail line.

"Why stop here?" said Kees. "We're almost there."

"The officers are afraid we're too spread out from the march," said Willem. "We'll set up camp here tonight and advance the rest of the way to the rail line in the morning."

Harm and Kees spent the night on picket duty. After digging a rifle pit, the two settled in for a long watchful night.

About midnight, Kees stirred. Harm looked up. "What?"

"Shhh. Listen."

Harm tilted his head. *Crack! Crack!* "Musket fire?"

"Axes," said Kees. "The rebels are chopping down trees. Probably putting up defensive works in front of the railroad. We should have attacked right away."

The chopping continued all night. Soldiers reported hearing it all up and down the picket line.

The next morning, the 25th Michigan prepared to advance. Spaced some twenty feet apart, Harm and his friends cautiously made their way into the trees that stood between them and the rail line.

Almost immediately, they took fire from Confederate skirmishers. Harm returned fire, then took cover behind an old stump. Several rebel musket balls embedded themselves in the other side of the stump. Harm's heart thumped as he reloaded. Would he ever get used to this?

The two lines traded fire all morning. Gradually, the 25th Michigan inched forward. Finally, the rebel skirmishers abandoned their positions and retreated to their main line. Harm and his friends pursued until they came under fire once more.

The rebels' main line was well positioned behind impressive defensive works made of freshly cut logs. In front of their works, they'd driven hundreds of logs into the earth and sharpened their exposed ends. The resulting abatis made a frontal attack all but impossible.

Kees couldn't hide his frustration. "We gave them all night to prepare for us."

When it became clear a frontal assault would not succeed, the 25th Michigan attempted a flanking maneuver. They followed the tracks for hours, but it was no use. The defensive works extended for miles in either direction.

Late in the day, the Union soldiers trudged back through the trees toward their camp. The creek lay on their right and a low stone wall on their left. Suddenly, they came under fire.

"What's this?" cried Kees.

Harm dove for cover behind a fallen tree. Rebel fire exploded from behind the stone wall.

Harm tried to return fire, but a hailstorm of musket balls rattled in the trees all around him. He waited until the sound died down, then rose to his knees. He looked for the regimental flag but couldn't find it.

A musket ball slapped the ground beside him, and he dropped back behind the fallen tree. When eventually the sound of the muskets died out again, Harm left the cover of his tree, but stayed low to the ground. He followed the creek back toward camp, dragging himself forward on his hands and knees.

It was full dark by the time he returned to camp. He wasn't sure what he would find there. Did the others make it back?

"There you are," said Kees, relief written all over his face. He shouted to Captain de Boe, "Harm's here. He's all right."

At the campfire, Ted and Gerrit and the others were all glad to see him. The regiment had become scattered in the midst of the skirmishing. Soldiers had been slowly returning in ones and twos for several hours.

Gerrit looked dejected. "They should be giving up by now. Instead, they fight like they still have a chance."

"Perhaps no one told them," said Ted.

"We missed our opportunity," said Kees. "Now it's too late—they've dug in."

Later, Willem joined them with more bad news. "We left our colors on the field today."

Harm's heart sank. "What happened?"

"Hard to say. The color-bearer fell early in the day. One of his guards picked up the flag and continued on. Later, he fell and a second guard took them up. Then we all came under fire and scrambled for cover. Somehow our colors were left behind."

Harm hated to think of their regimental flag, the colors that had encouraged them in every battle from Tebbs Bend to Atlanta, left on the field, or maybe even in enemy hands.

"What now?" asked Gerrit.

"We go home?" offered Ted.

"No way," said Kees. "Tomorrow morning, we go back and get our colors back."

Kees awoke the next morning with more talk of a glorious raid. But when he emerged from his tent, he stopped in his tracks. "What's this?"

Their regimental flag stood right where it belonged. It was tattered and torn, but boldly declared the 25th Michigan was still in the fight.

Willem filled them in. In the middle of the night, Ben van Raalte, oldest son of Rev. van Raalte, had crept back to the battlefield, retrieved the flag, and returned it to camp.

Everyone gathered around Ben, congratulating him. Harm slapped him on the back. "Well done."

Kees congratulated him, too. But back at his tent, he grumbled, "I should have thought of that. They'll probably give him a medal."

When it became clear they could not capture the rail line, the 25th Michigan was called back to the northern outskirts of Atlanta.

Willem volunteered to transport supplies from a nearby depot and asked Harm to join him. The next morning, they climbed into a wagon and rolled out of camp.

Willem drove the mules like an expert. They rode all morning, picked up the supplies and turned back toward Atlanta. As they made their way back to camp, they came upon hundreds of people walking by the side of the road.

Harm looked closer. Men and women, boys and girls, some carrying bundles, many with nothing but the clothes on their backs. "Where are they going?"

Willem shrugged. "Sometimes they follow the army."

Harm heard someone playing a musical instrument. He scanned the crowd and spotted a young man playing an odd-looking guitar. Harm said, "Stop the wagon."

Willem drew up the mules, and Harm leapt to the ground, making his way toward the music.

The man saw Harm coming and stopped playing. He stood shirtless with a bundle at his feet, eyeing Harm cautiously. His guitar-like instrument had a circular head with a skin drawn tight over it, like a drum.

"I'm Harm," he said, offering his hand. "Harm van Wyke."

The man ignored Harm's hand. "Mose. Just Mose."

"What kind of guitar is that?" asked Harm.

"It's a banjo."

"You pluck the strings?"

"First the thumb, then the fingers." He demonstrated. The sound was sharp, almost harsh, but Harm liked it.

The rest of the throng trudged on toward Atlanta.

"I don't want to make you fall behind your friends," said Harm.

"I have no friends here," said Mose.

"Family?"

"I have a sister in Charleston. I'm going there to find her."

"It's a long way," said Harm.

Mose shrugged. "Too far for family?"

Harm nodded that he understood.

As Harm stood there, Mose played a tune with a bold and driving rhythm, and began to sing. Harm didn't catch all the words, but concluded quickly it was no hymn. Someone got murdered. Someone got away with it.

When Mose finished, he turned to swing his sack up onto his shoulder.

Harm drew a sharp breath. Mose' back was crisscrossed with deep and ugly scars.

Mose caught the look in Harm's eyes. "Master Evans and me, we disagreed time to time."

Harm trembled to think of the brutal whippings that would leave such scars.

"Once I stole a chicken. Once he caught me with a Bible. Master Evans don't allow his slaves to read."

Harm had a hard time comprehending that. In his own home and throughout the *Kolonie*, the ability to read was highly valued.

He looked at Mose, "Not even the Bible?"

"Not even a sack of seeds."

"But you know about the Bible?"

"I know what the Bible says. My Pap taught me that."

"Then you know it's important."

Mose's eyes narrowed. "I'll tell you what I know. Master Evans, he read the Bible every day. Went to church twice on Sunday."

Harm waited uncomfortably.

"Then he come home and beat me half to death for dropping a sack of seed on the ground. That's what I know about the Bible."

Harm felt a stab of shame. It was true, what Rev. van Raalte said. When those who profess to love God live in hatred against their neighbor, they give occasion for others to despise God's name.

He offered the man a ride in the wagon as far as Atlanta, but Mose refused.

Back at the wagon, Harm asked, "What will become of all these people?"

Willem touched the reins and the wagon began to roll. "The army sets up camps for them. Contraband camps. They provide food and shelter. Not much else."

Upon their return to camp, Harm learned that Dirk van Raalte, Ben's younger brother, had been injured.

"He was delivering a message," said Kees. "Rebels got him in the arm."

"Bad?"

"They had to take his right arm at the shoulder."

Harm groaned. "Can we see him?"

"They sent him to a hospital outside Atlanta. Ben is on his way to visit him."

Weeks passed, and not much changed as the Union Army laid siege to the city and waited. A dozen cannons stood just beyond their camp, pounding the city night and day with twelve-pound shells.

Then, one night, Harm awoke to a series of earth-shaking explosions. He scrambled from his tent, grabbed his musket, and fell into battle formation.

Over the city, flames leapt toward the heavens. The roar of the fire was so intense Harm could hear it even at a distance.

"Form up," ordered Captain de Boe. "We've got orders to advance."

Ted turned to Harm. "Advance?"

The 25th Michigan crept forward, expecting Confederate fire at any moment, but none came. Upon reaching the outermost defensive positions, they found them abandoned.

"They've pulled back," said Kees. "Come on." He pushed forward. Harm and the others followed, content to let Kees lead the way.

They reached more Confederate positions, all abandoned. Eventually, they entered the streets of the city. Kees pointed out a blackened railyard. Dozens of box cars still smoldered. Structures for blocks in every direction were covered with ash.

"Looks like a munitions warehouse blew up," said Gerrit. "Do our cannons reach this far?"

Willem shook his head. "It's just like we saw outside Knoxville. They're withdrawing from the city and they can't get their munitions out, so they chose to destroy them."

"Along with half the city," said Ted.

As it became clear Atlanta had fallen, Union soldiers began to celebrate. They broke into stores, stealing whatever they wanted. They passed bottles of whiskey amongst themselves. One soldier tied a rag to his bayonet and poked it into a pile of coals. The rag caught fire, and he waved it about victoriously. Then he strode to a nearby building and held the burning rag up to an awning. The awning caught fire, and flames leapt into the air.

Soon, other buildings erupted in flames as well. Smoke billowed through the streets, stinging Harm's eyes. He was relieved when his company was called back outside the city.

Kees blamed the rebels. "You heard those explosions. They did most of the damage before we ever got there."

Harm didn't respond, but he knew what he'd seen. He was thankful to stay outside the city in the weeks that followed.

In early October, Harm received two letters from home. The first was from his family. They expressed gratitude to God for his health and safety. The weather was sunny and warm. The harvest was safely in and plentiful. Harm checked the envelope carefully to see if there was any news about Ted's father. Nothing. Maybe things were getting better with him.

The second letter was from Sarah.

*Holland, Michigan*
*October 1, 1864*

*Dear Harm,*

*Thank you so much for your most recent letter. It is always good to hear from you. Please know I look forward to your letters and treasure them when they come. I continue to pray for you daily, and think of you even more.*

*Your drawing of the Georgia pine trees now hangs on my bedroom wall. I like it very much. Two of my sisters, Rebekah and Leah, share my room with me. They demand drawings of their own. Rebekah thinks a fast-moving stream tumbling over rocks and boulders would be nice. Leah will accept nothing but a prancing steed.*

*I write this under the big maple tree in front of my house. It is already turning red and orange. The days have been warm and sunny, the nights clear and cool. The war drags on and the winter looms near, but I pray you will return with the first warm winds of spring.*

*I keep all of your letters and often re-read them. I cannot help but notice that you rarely mention the war. I realize you see much pain and sorrow. I understand, too, your desire to shield me from the horrors of war.*

*But please understand, I am not as fragile as all that. If I were, how could I survive here? I was with my cousin Tess when she received word of the death of her beloved husband. I can still hear her shrieks and inconsolable sobs. I see the emptiness behind her eyes. As for smells, I changed her little Cora and ewwhhh! I joke, but as they say, sometimes it is either laugh or cry.*

*I ask that you share your burdens as I have freely shared my sorrow at the loss of my dear brother, Howard. You have been an encouragement to me and I wish to be a help to you as well. Perhaps I ask too much. Nonetheless, I ask.*

*My prayer continues that God may keep you safe and return you to me.*

Sarah

———

Harm wasn't sure he could write about the war, but decided to do his best to honor her request.

Later that day, Spencer and Clay stopped by Harm's tent. Harm was glad to see them. He asked Spencer what he knew about contraband camps.

"Not much," said Spencer. "They're temporary camps for those who've gained freedom from slavery. Chaplains and missionary societies help provide food and shelter. Sometimes even schools. But there's never enough money. Some are more like prison camps—overcrowded, lots of disease. Why do you ask?"

Harm explained about Mose.

"I wish I'd been there," said Clay.

"We're going into the city to find a bookseller," said Spencer. "We thought maybe you'd join us."

Harm shook his head. "No, thanks. I've seen enough of Atlanta."

Willem agreed to go. A few minutes later, he and Spencer set off for the city.

Clay decided to stay behind with Harm. Later, Ted joined them. They warmed up a pot of coffee and talked about home. Ted asked Clay about growing up in Kalamazoo.

He shrugged. "It's like any other town, I guess."

Harm sipped his coffee. "Is it true you were living on the streets?"

"My parents died of smallpox when I was young. My Uncle took me in, but he didn't treat me so good, especially when he drank."

Harm glanced at Ted. "Whiskey can do that."

Ted nodded. "So I've heard."

"What will you do when the war is over?" asked Harm. "Go back to school?"

"Maybe. I can read and write. I was never too good at sums, though."

Harm smiled. "They come in useful. Don't give up."

"That's what Spencer says. One of the reasons he wanted to go into the city was to get me a book on practical arithmetic."

"Why didn't you go with him?"

"I prefer stories. I hoped you'd tell me some more Bible stories."

Harm looked at Ted. "Any suggestions?"

"You could start at the beginning."

Harm agreed and told Clay the creation story: how God said, 'Let there be light' and there was light. How he spoke everything into being in the same way—sky and oceans and land, stars and fish and trees. But how when he made man, he took dust from the ground, formed it into a man, and breathed into him the breath of life.

"That was Adam?"

"It was. The name Adam means 'from the earth.' Then God took a rib from Adam and made Eve. Her name means 'of the man.'"

Clay puzzled over that. "Why didn't God just say 'Let there be people?'"

"Good question. Maybe to show we're different from other creatures. I think that's why he breathed life into Adam too—to show we have the life of heaven in us. God created Adam and Eve in his image, to be his own children."

"Then what?"

"They turned against him." Harm told about the garden of Eden, the tree of life and the tree of the knowledge of good and evil. Adam and Eve listened to the lie of the devil, disobeyed God and ate of the forbidden fruit, bringing sin and death into all of creation.

"And smallpox?" asked Clay.

"And war," said Ted.

Harm nodded. "But that's not the end. Even though they turned against God, he still loved them. He sent his son to free them from the power of the devil."

"That was Jesus."

"It was."

Some time later, Spencer and Willem returned from the city. Harm noticed they were empty-handed. "The stores are boarded up," said Willem.

Spencer sighed. "I'm so tired of destruction." He sat down. "I've been trying to leave the past behind me, but I can't stop thinking about Cassville. Now, this."

Harm didn't know what to say. He still thought about Cassville, too.

Spencer and Clay rose to go. Spencer glanced at Harm. "I'd hate to think God could put an end to all this and chooses not to."

Harm pressed his lips together, searching for the right words. Finally, he said, "He has a purpose in everything. Right now, that includes this war. I'm not saying I understand it. But would it be better if he wanted to stop the war and couldn't? If he wanted peace but was powerless to do anything about it?"

Spencer weighed that, then smiled. "No, Harm. It wouldn't. But I still don't see how any good can come from this."

"He's got a point," said Willem. "Who exactly is benefitting from this war?"

"I don't see it either," said Harm, "not right now. But that doesn't mean it isn't true. Maybe the war will end slavery. Maybe it will save the Union. Maybe it will bring a lifetime of peace and prosperity once it's over."

"That's a lot of maybes," said Spencer.

"You're right. But this much I know—*everything* serves God's purpose to save his people. This war, too."

Spencer nodded to acknowledge he understood Harm, but didn't respond. Instead, he rose to his feet and motioned for Clay to join him. "Sorry, Harm, we've got to get back."

After they'd gone, Harm went for a walk to be alone. He felt exhausted, like his long absence from home and church were taking a toll on him. He longed to worship with like-minded believers again, praising God with one heart and one mind and one voice. He remembered all of the psalms where King David had expressed those same longings.

That night, when the soldiers from Holland gathered for devotions, Harm read Psalm 84, focusing on verse 2: *"My soul longeth, yea, even fainteth for the courts of the* Lord: *my heart and my flesh crieth out for the living God."*

Together, they sang Psalm 65, where David spoke of his desire for God's house.

*There, in thy holy habitation*
*Thou wilt thy saints provide*
*With every blessing of salvation*
*Till all are satisfied.*

Later in his tent, Harm's mind returned to his conversation with Spencer. He welcomed questions about God's sovereignty from Spencer, but was troubled when Willem joined in. Willem should know better. It struck Harm then, how much time Willem spent with Spencer. How could Willem *not* be influenced by Spencer's skepticism? And *he* had introduced them.

## CHAPTER 34

# OCTOBER 1864

In the Tillema's tidy home on Eleventh Street, the three oldest sisters, Sarah, Rebekah, and Leah, were busy making pies—sour cherry, peach, and apple. The younger sisters, June, Mary, and Rose, had spent the morning helping to prepare the fruit, but were sent out to play as the older girls prepared the dough.

Mrs. Tillema kept a watchful eye on the proceedings, but her daughters knew their roles well and went about them with quiet efficiency.

Mr. Tillema knew enough to get out of his house on pie day. "I'll be back in a bit," he assured them as he turned to go. "Save me some cherries."

Sarah flicked flour at him, and Rebekah slapped his hand when he tried to steal a cherry.

By the time Mr. Tillema returned, a dozen pies lay cooling in the windows.

He held a letter addressed to his oldest daughter. The first time a letter had arrived with Harm van Wyke's handwriting, it announced his only son had been injured in the fighting. Then came the letter announcing his death. Still, Mr. Tillema liked Harm. He slipped the letter into Sarah's hand.

She clasped it to her breast and slipped out the door while her sisters argued over how long they had to let the pies cool before they could cut into one. Sarah seated herself at the base of the big maple tree and opened the envelope.

———

Atlanta, Georgia
October 10, 1864

Dear Sarah,

Thank you for your letter dated October 1, which I received on the 8th. It was so good to hear from you. I know exactly which maple tree you spoke of. It is always the first to green in the spring and the first to show color in the autumn. Perhaps, as you suggest, we will enjoy next summer in its shade.

———

She stopped reading and gazed up into the overspreading branches. She tried to imagine him sitting there beside her. How could she possibly wait until summer?

———

I've enclosed a drawing of Mill Creek for Rebekah. For Leah's, I will have to find a more promising model than the mules we keep here.

———

She smiled and drew out the picture. It was just what Rebekah had requested. She would love it.

———

You ask me to share my burden. I will try. We have battled the Confederate Army nearly every day since June—at Etowah River, Kingston, Allatoona Pass, then in the mountains. They have taken the lives of many friends and acquaintances. We have taken their lives as well. Ever since Cassville I have struggled with the senselessness of it all. It is one thing to confess man's depravity, another to experience it day after day without reprieve. I hesitate to speak of the disfigured, the dismembered, the stench of disease, the cries of the dying.

———

Sarah hardly breathed as she read Harm's words. She could feel his pain and also his hesitancy to say too much. She blinked back tears.

———

I realize the burdens of war are not limited to soldiers. Each time I am confronted with death, I am reminded of the loss of Howard. I think of the pain that you and your family must bear, not only now, but into the future. It hurts me to think of you in pain. Perhaps that is saying too much. But I have said it.

I'm sorry if this sounds very depressing. We do not spend our days in sackcloth and ashes. We go forward in faith and hope. Kees makes sure we still have fun. Ted makes sure we laugh. But no matter what we do or where we go, a sense of emptiness lingers.

———

She lowered the letter and held it in her lap. Somehow, Harm had managed to put into words the very feelings she experienced almost daily. She and her sisters, even her parents, had managed to resume a sort of normal life. They played games. They baked pies. But always in the back of her mind was the realization that Howard would not return from the war. And sometimes guilt—if she managed to go a whole day without thinking of him, was she being disloyal?

She picked up the letter again and continued to read.

———

General Sherman has secured the city and talk has turned to what will come next. Some say we will join General Grant in his assault on Richmond. Some say we will march all the way to the sea. Some say we will remain here until we defeat General Hood and his army. We put our trust in God and wait on his good providence. With Atlanta fallen, I am hopeful the war will end soon.

One other thing I will write, only because it weighs on me. When I joined the infantry the plight of the slaves was not foremost in my mind. I was pleased when President Lincoln freed them, but understood it was, in part, a political calculation. Since then, I have crossed paths with some of them. Not often. But enough to see that Rev. van Raalte was clear-eyed in his condemnation of slavery.

Please write again, and soon. I value your letters above all others. May God bless you with every good thing.

Love, Harm

---

Sarah placed the letter back in the envelope and returned to the house. Avoiding the commotion in the kitchen, she went straight to her bedroom and placed the envelope and letter in the box where she kept all his letters.

Rebekah slipped through the door to join her. "Did he write anything terribly romantic?"

"He said he values my letters above all others."

"Oh, I *like* him. What did he say about the war?"

"He's hopeful it will end soon."

"Father doesn't think so."

"He didn't say he *thinks* so. He said he's hopeful. Oh, and he sent this for you."

Rebekah admired Harm's drawing. "Oh, he *is* sweet. You better marry him."

## CHAPTER 35

# OCTOBER 1864 – JANUARY 1865

With Atlanta secured, General Sherman determined to march across Georgia to the Atlantic Ocean. But first, he detached the Army of the Ohio, including the 25th Michigan, and sent them to finish off General John B. Hood, who was marching what remained of his Army of Tennessee toward Nashville.

Trying to get ahead of General Hood, the Army of the Ohio retraced their steps back through Northern Georgia into East Tennessee, then made their way west toward Nashville.

About that time, the army reinstated Colonel Moore as commander of the brigade that included the 25th Michigan. Harm and his friends were thrilled. Back in Kalamazoo, the colonel had welcomed the volunteers from Holland warmly. With a firm and patient hand, he had taught them to work together as a company and as a regiment. He had taught them to fight.

Colonel Moore made clear he was happy to be back, but refused to discuss the details of his return.

Rumors spread like wildfire. "I heard President Lincoln got personally involved," said Kees. "He forced General Boyle to return Colonel Moore to command."

Major Harrod also rejoined the brigade, though without celebration.

The regiment marched long days as they hurried to the defense of Nashville. Along the way, they learned President Lincoln had won re-election.

"Yes!" said Kees. "This war is over."

"Make sure they tell General Lee," said Ted.

In November, they battled with Confederate troops near Franklin, Tennessee. From there, they marched north toward Nashville. A cold rain fell, turning the roads to mud. They marched all day and set up camp in the gathering gray of evening.

At roll call, a group of stragglers had not yet arrived.

"I heard Otto is one of the missing," said Willem.

Kees' face went white. "Otto Boot?"

Everyone knew Otto's parents were friends with Kees' parents. Gerrit put a hand on Kees' shoulder. "They might have stopped to get out of the rain, or maybe they joined up with another brigade."

Harm nodded. That happened sometimes. And he didn't want to think the worst either.

Colonel Moore sent out volunteers from the cavalry to look for the missing soldiers, but Kees wasn't satisfied. He took Harm aside. "They don't know Otto. They'll ride around for an hour and then give up."

"What else can we do?" asked Harm.

"I'm thinking of going after him."

"How will we find him?" Harm had already made up his mind to join Kees if he decided to go. After all, Kees had risked his life to help rescue Howard.

"I haven't figured that out yet," said Kees. "But there's got to be a way."

"If the cavalry can't find them on horseback, it'll be hard for us on foot."

Kees considered that. "You're right. We'd never find him. I just hate to do nothing."

"The cavalry is out there. They'll find him."

Harm stayed up late, hoping for word of Otto and the others, but no news came. When he finally went to bed, he noticed Kees wasn't in his tent. And even after making a quick circuit around the camp, Harm didn't find him.

He woke Ted. "Have you seen Kees?"

Ted rubbed his eyes. "Not since I fell asleep."

"I can't find him."

"Did you check Charlie Marley's?"

Harm groaned. He made his way to the camp of the 80th Indiana. Charlie and his friends were playing cards. They hadn't seen Kees.

That left only one explanation—Kees had gone looking for Otto. Alone. Harm returned to his tent, but couldn't sleep. Otto and the others might have been captured by rebels. Kees might be walking into a trap. Should Harm report his absence to Captain de Boe? To Colonel Moore? If he did, Kees would get the stockade for sure. Unless they shot him as a deserter.

Harm rose well before dawn and made his way to the gate. He asked the guards if the cavalry had returned.

A burly private nodded his head. "An hour ago."

"Did they find anything?"

"Nothing."

"How about you?" asked Harm. "Have you seen anything unusual?"

"Unusual? No. They did say one of the horses went missing."

Harm returned to his tent and waited. At least Kees wasn't on foot.

Finally, the bugle played *reveille* and the camp began to stir. Harm tried to act normally, but his heart pounded in his chest as his company gathered for roll call. Soon they would discover Kees was missing.

When Captain de Boe got to Kees' name he looked around. "Kees?"

No reply.

"Kees de Groot?"

Silence.

The captain turned to Harm. "Any idea where Kees is this morning?"

Harm's mind raced. "He . . . ahhh—"

"I'm here!" Kees crashed through some bushes nearby and stumbled into formation. His hair was a mess, and his left sleeve was torn. He caught Harm's eye and gave a grim shake of his head. Otto was still missing.

Captain de Boe glanced at Kees, opened his mouth as if to say something more, then shook his head and continued with roll call.

Later, Kees filled Harm in. He'd borrowed a horse and spent the night searching the countryside without success. At one point, he'd stumbled on the cavalry search party and barely escaped capture.

"Why'd you leave without me?" asked Harm. "I was planning to go with you."

"I know. I didn't want to turn you into a horse thief. Besides, no use in both of us getting shot."

They waited several more days, gradually losing hope Otto would be found. Then one day, Willem brought stunning news. Oliver Blanchard, one of the soldiers who'd gone missing, had made it back to camp.

"Where's he been?" asked Kees. "What about the others?"

"Let me tell it," said Willem. "A wagon dropped him off at the gate this morning. I was with Major Harrod when they brought him in. Oliver said he and a dozen others fell behind on the march. They were crossing a creek just at dusk when thirty-some bushwhackers charged up on them. They stole their money and forced them to take off their boots and caps. They split them up and marched them into a wooded area. At the top of a ravine, they stopped and shot them."

"How did he survive?" asked Harm.

"He must have fainted just as they fired. The ball grazed the top of his head. He woke up in the middle of the night and crawled out of the woods. The next morning, a farmer discovered him in his field. He took him home and took care of him until he was well enough to return to camp."

"What about the others?" asked Kees.

"They're all dead. Otto, too."

Kees closed his eyes and turned away.

Harm hung his head. Another son of Holland who wouldn't return to the *Kolonie* after the war.

The next day at mail call, Harm received two letters, one from his family and one from Sarah. She thanked him for his letter. It had been hard to read about Cassville and Atlanta, but she was glad to gain a sense of the things that troubled him.

He sat down and wrote her another long letter. He found he could tell her things he didn't even share with his family.

The next morning, they resumed their march toward Nashville. They marched near the middle of their brigade with other regiments to their left and right.

As they made their way through a notch between two hills, the other regiments bunched in on them from either side. Carefully organized lines twisted into a confusion of soldiers. The whole knot of them came to a halt at the base of a large grassy hill while officers tried to sort things out.

Kees pointed toward the top of the hill.

Harm followed his eyes and saw a number of horses appear, then draw back.

Ted saw it, too. "Cavalry?"

Kees shook his head. "Worse. Artillery."

As he spoke, a cannon thundered from beyond the crest of the hill. A shell whistled over their heads, landing behind their line and exploding in dirt and debris.

Harm never heard an order to advance, but the entire brigade burst up the hill. A second shell exploded, much nearer than the first. Harm raced up the hill, stumbled, and rose again, not sure what he'd find at the top. Kees reached the crest first and immediately came under fire. He dropped to the ground, but continued to scramble forward. Harm followed his lead.

Beyond the crest of the hill was a slight depression, then a rise to another hill, this one heavily wooded toward the top. The Confederate soldiers had dug in at the tree line.

Orders came for the Union soldiers to advance. Muskets blazed. Cannons roared. Confederate soldiers held the high ground but were badly outnumbered. After an hour of fierce battle, the rebels withdrew into the trees.

Harm's brigade pursued them. At the same time, other regiments closed in on the rebel flanks.

The fighting continued for another day, but by the end of the battle, the Confederate Army of Tennessee had ceased to be a threat. Whole regiments dissolved as Confederate soldiers slipped away and returned to their homes.

"The Confederacy can't hold out much longer," said Kees.

"General Grant is marching on Richmond from the north and General Sherman is carving up Georgia."

Harm agreed. It was only a matter of time. But how much time? And how many more must die?

The defeat of the Confederate Army of Tennessee left the 25th Michigan with little to do and little idea what would come next. Harm suspected they would soon go east, but didn't know where or when.

A week later, on Christmas Eve, Harm and his friends gathered around a roaring fire for devotions. Ted read the Christmas story from Luke 2, focusing on verse 13 and 14: *"And suddenly there was with the angel a multitude of the heavenly host praising God, and saying, Glory to God in the highest, and on earth peace, good will toward men."*

"On earth peace—that sounds good," sighed Kees.

"It's peace from *spiritual* warfare," said Gerrit. "The warfare we know is only a picture of the spiritual—ever since Adam and Eve, we've rebelled against God's will."

"But Jesus changed that," said Kees. "He made it possible for us to go to heaven."

"Still," noted Harm, "the angels spoke of peace on *earth*."

Gerrit nodded. "We enjoy peace with God already now by faith. It isn't perfect. But it's real."

Their discussion turned to other earthly pictures that pointed to Christ.

"Nearly everything in the Old Testament," said Gerrit. "Moses and the exodus. He led Israel out of slavery in Egypt."

"God made him a mediator between himself and his people."

"And Joshua, too. He led Israel into Canaan—the land of rest."

"What about Aaron? He was a priest."

"Really all of the prophets, priests, and kings."

"But especially David. He was a conquering king."

"And Solomon. He reigned over a kingdom of peace."

"It wasn't just people, either. Think of the tabernacle, and the temple. God dwelled with his people."

"And all of the sacrifices."

"And the feasts, too."

"Right. Especially the Passover."

"And the Great Day of Atonement."

Eventually, talk died down, and Gerrit said, "Our third Christmas away. Next year we'll be home."

"Maybe," said Willem.

"Definitely. Our three years are up in September."

"Suppose the war keeps going?" countered Willem. "We should re-enlist."

"We've done our part," said Gerrit.

"And then some," agreed Ted.

Kees put more wood on the fire. "I think this war is over. We'll be home in a month."

Willem shook his head. "It's not done in the east. Besides, we've got a lot to learn yet. I'd like to see Baltimore. Maybe even New York."

Ted warmed his hands over the flames. "We've seen Munfordville."

Willem rolled his eyes. "Someplace important."

"We've seen Atlanta," said Kees. "Is that important enough for you?"

"Someplace still standing," said Ted.

Taps ended their devotions for the night.

The following Sunday, Harm and his friends had opportunity to worship in a small church outside of Nashville. As soon as they entered the building, they felt the eyes of the members upon them.

They were simple farmers and shopkeepers, but they were also Confederates with no love for Yankee soldiers. Some glared at the four boys, eyes filled with hostility. Others ignored them. A few, moved by Christian charity or Southern hospitality, made a point of greeting them. Polite, but aloof.

The minister, barely thirty and filled with zeal, read from Matthew 28. He drew out all of the vowel sounds in a lyrical drawl as he spoke of Jesus' command to teach all nations, baptizing them in the name of the Father, and of the Son, and of the Holy Ghost. He spoke of missionaries in foreign lands. He urged his congregation to share the gospel of Jesus Christ with their neighbors at every opportunity. He didn't emphasize the Holy Spirit's role in turning sinners to God, but Harm was pleased when he noted that only in Jesus' power could their witness have any effect.

One benefit of attending church again turned out to be the singing. The hymns were unfamiliar, but the congregation sang with enthusiasm, and the experience left Harm thrilled. The final hymn, "Amazing Grace," was especially beautiful.

*Amazing grace! How sweet the sound*
*That saved a wretch like me.*
*I once was lost, but now am found;*
*Was blind, but now I see.*

The third stanza sent shivers down Harm's spine. The words seemed to have been written especially for him.

*Through many dangers, toils and snares*
*I have already come;*
*'Tis grace hath brought me safe thus far*
*And grace will lead me home.*

Harm and his friends had come through many dangers, toils, and snares. And they took comfort in the knowledge that the same grace which had brought them safe thus far would lead them home.

The final stanza of the hymn spoke of heaven, and again Harm was moved at the beauty of its expression.

*When we've been there ten thousand years,*
*Bright shining as the sun,*
*We've no less days to sing God's praise*
*Than when we'd first begun.*

Harm was in no hurry to leave after the service, but Kees said, "We should go before someone works up the courage to confront us."

They moved to go, but the pastor stopped them at the door. "I'm glad you could join us this morning. God is no respecter of persons, and the good news doesn't stop at borders."

Harm thanked him and mentioned that he had enjoyed the final hymn.

"Ah, yes." The pastor glanced over his shoulder, then lowered his voice. "Not all our members would be pleased to hear it, but the author of that particular hymn, a Mr. John Newton, was a reformed slave trader who became an abolitionist."

Harm looked at him, surprised.

The pastor smiled slyly and put a finger to his lips.

The next day, the brigade received orders to travel east to Washington with a view to rejoining General Sherman's forces in Georgia. They marched eighty miles in eight days to Clifton, where they boarded a paddlewheel steamer, the *A. Baker*. Over a dozen steamers, including gunboats, brought the brigade down the Tennessee River, then up the Ohio River toward the east.

Life on the river seemed like a long, slow dream—no drill, no marching, no skirmishing, and regular meals besides. The weather turned mild. Soldiers sat on deck and watched the countryside roll by. They talked about old times. They talked about the war. They talked about what would come after the war.

Kees leaned back on his chair. "I'm not sure I can handle working in my father's warehouse for the rest of my life."

"Then do something else," said Ted.

Kees grinned. "I had this idea—we could go out west and be cowboys."

Harm raised an eyebrow, and Kees laughed. "Let me finish. I mean if we can find a good Reformed church, of course."

"There are churches everywhere," said Willem. "They're not *that* different. We're not the only ones going to heaven, you know."

"But we should join the best church we can find," insisted Gerrit. "We should put that ahead of everything else. You know, 'Seek ye first the kingdom of God.'"

Kees nodded. "But if they don't have one out there, couldn't we start one?"

"We could," said Harm. "I hope we do. Colorado. California . . ."

"They already have one in Pella," offered Ted.

Kees looked confused, "What's Pella?"

"It doesn't matter," said Willem. "There's still a war to fight. That's why we're going east."

"We'll see." Kees rocked back on his chair. "I think we've fired our last round."

Harm hoped Kees was right, but couldn't shake the fear that the last days of the war might be the hardest.

After several days on the river, the *A. Baker* reached Louisville. Harm and his friends stood on deck as they rolled past their old camp, reminiscing about their time there.

"We should stop in and see our old chaplain," said Kees. "Seems he decided he could serve us best by staying in Louisville."

"Fitting, though," said Ted. "What good's a bread preacher when we had no bread?"

While docked in Louisville, Harm suggested they gather everyone for devotions. He invited Spencer and Clay as well.

Clay agreed immediately. Spencer said, "We'll see." In the end, they both showed up.

Harm read Psalm 40, focusing on verses 1 and 2: "*I waited patiently for the LORD; and he inclined unto me, and heard my cry. He brought me up also out of an horrible pit, out of the miry clay, and set my feet upon a rock, and established my goings.*"

Clay grinned when Harm got to the part about miry clay.

"We know God hears our prayers," said Gerrit. "But that's been especially comforting in hard times like we've seen."

"That's true," said Kees. "But it's hard when his answer isn't what we want to hear. Like with Otto."

"Sometimes he doesn't seem to answer at all," said Ted.

"He always answers," insisted Gerrit. "But like David, sometimes we have to wait patiently."

Kees winced. "I'm not so good at waiting."

Spencer cleared his throat. They all looked at him. He smiled, sheepishly. "I know you didn't invite me here to disagree with you . . ."

"But . . ." said Ted.

"Well, I used to pray. I prayed every day when I was younger. But I never saw that it made any difference. Do you think God truly hears you?"

"Yes," said Gerrit.

"How can you know?"

Gerrit held up his Bible. "Psalm 40."

Spencer sighed. "Besides that?"

"We have God's word. Do we need more?"

"Even then," argued Spencer. "David was a king. Maybe God heard *him*. But we're just a bunch of volunteers. The army doesn't even care about us."

"The Bible says God cares for even the sparrows."

"That's true. But I've seen sparrows snatched by an owl and crushed in a moment."

"That's not . . ." sputtered Gerrit. "That's . . ."

"We're not saying life is easy," said Harm. "Friends die. Family, too. We know that. But that doesn't mean God doesn't care. It's just . . ."

Clay jumped in. "It's because of Adam and Eve."

They all looked at him. "That's right," said Harm. "We don't blame God for sin and death. We did that to ourselves."

"But Jesus overcame that for his people," said Gerrit. "He turns the evil we face in this life to our good."

Spencer didn't seem convinced. "So, being away from home all this time is for your good? What about your friends who died? I just don't see it."

Harm thought of Howard and his grieving family back home. "We don't see it all the time either. But we believe God keeps his word. That's faith, I guess."

Spencer stayed for about an hour, then excused himself politely. The others talked and prayed and sang psalms deep into the night.

The next day, the steamers left Louisville and continued up the Ohio River. After they were on their way, Clay came to see Harm and Ted.

"Did you enjoy our devotions?" asked Ted.

"I did. Why do you sing in Dutch?"

Ted laughed. "At home we speak Dutch, too."

Clay asked for a story about Jesus, and Harm told him how one day Jesus passed by a man who had been blind since his birth. Jesus spit on the ground and made clay out of the dirt. Then he put it on the man's eyes.

Clay's eyes lit up. "Does the Bible say 'clay?'"

"It does. Then Jesus had him wash it off and when he did, he wasn't blind anymore. He could see."

"Is that true?"

"It is. It was a miracle. Jesus isn't just a man. He's the Son of God."

"What other miracles did he do?"

"Once he changed six big barrels of water into wine. Another time he fed five thousand people with just five loaves of bread and two fish."

"And he rose from the dead," said Ted.

Harm agreed. "The leaders arrested him, and soldiers nailed him to a cross. He died there. He was even buried. But on the third day, he rose from the dead. He appeared to his followers and then went up into heaven."

The weather continued to be mild as the riverboat made its way east. Harm sat on the deck and wrote letters to all of his loved ones at home.

Eventually, they approached their last stop on the river, Cincinnati. Harm and his friends gathered for one last time of devotions before leaving the steamer. The night had turned colder, but they still decided to meet outside on the deck. Clay joined them again, but not Spencer.

Gerrit read 2 Corinthians 6, focusing on verses 14-16: *"Be ye not unequally yoked together with unbelievers: for what fellowship hath righteousness with unrighteousness? and what com-*

*munion hath light with darkness? and what concord hath Christ with Belial? or what part hath he that believeth with an infidel? and what agreement hath the temple of God with idols? for ye are the temple of the living God; as God hath said, I will dwell in them, and walk in them; and I will be their God, and they shall be my people."*

"We're supposed to be a light in the darkness," said Kees. "I can't say I've lived up to that."

Harm nodded. "None of us have. I think of all the times I've fallen short."

Kees hung his head. "That's mostly my fault. I'm sorry about that. I keep dragging people into trouble."

"Kicking and screaming," said Ted.

Harm thought of Rev van Raalte's words. "It's hard being in the world, but not of it."

Gerrit crossed his arms. "But that's no excuse."

"It's not too late," said Kees. "It would be nice to go home and not be ashamed of our time in the army. I know I've fallen short. But you know . . ." He would have gone on, but suddenly the night sky filled with snowflakes. Kees jumped to his feet and ran about the deck trying to catch them on his tongue.

Gerrit wasn't amused. He turned to Harm and Ted. "I can't believe you're going to let him get away with that."

"Eating snowflakes?" said Ted.

"He breaks all the rules like they don't apply to him. Now he's sorry and we're supposed to forgive him?"

Ted considered that. "Isn't that what Jesus does with us?"

"He'll just go and do the same things again tomorrow."

"Isn't that what we do?" asked Ted.

"It's not the same."

"It's *just* the same," said Harm, frustrated with Gerrit's attitude.

"How often did Jesus say we should forgive each other? Seventy times seven?"

"That's different," snapped Gerrit.

"How? We all need forgiveness."

"Not like Kees."

"Just like Kees," said Harm. "With him, everything is out in the open. But I know what goes on in my mind. I need forgiveness every bit as much as he does."

Gerrit sat stone-faced.

"And *you* do, too," said Harm. "If you don't think so, reread your Catechism."

## CHAPTER 36

# JANUARY 1865

The clouds hung low over the van Wyke farm, and the wind howled icy cold.

Mother sat in her bedroom with Father, who'd taken to his sickbed. Earlier in the week, he'd come down with chills and a fever.

Trina stirred a pot of stew on the stove and kept one eye on a loaf of bread. It was her first time in charge of the bread, and she wanted it to be perfect.

She asked Sam's opinion. "Is it ready?"

"It looks ready. It smells ready."

It did smell good. And the crust was golden brown.

Mother returned to the kitchen to wet a cloth and returned to Father's side.

Later, when Father was sleeping again, she took her place at the table. She tried to act unconcerned, but Sam and Trina knew better. When they finished eating, Sam read a passage from the Bible and closed with prayer.

Then Mother read aloud the latest letter from Harm.

Cincinnati, Ohio

January 13, 1865

Dear Father, Mother, and family at home,

The Army of Tennessee is no more! They gave us a battle at Franklin in November and again in Nashville a few days ago but it seems they will battle no more.

I pray this finds you healthy and well. I am as strong as ever. Thank you for your letter of January 2, which I received today.

By now you have heard the sad story of Otto Boot. We grieve as we are once again reminded this life is but a vapor.

We have come by steamship from Tennessee and are enjoying the respite from the war immensely. We are curious to see our nation's capital. I'll let you know if we see the president. From Washington we will be sent to join General Grant in Virginia or General Sherman in Georgia.

Father, is there any news in the church? Who are the new elders? Were you nominated?

Mother, we recently had an opportunity to worship in a church near Nashville. The singing was a delight. It was good to see that even people divided by war can unite in worship.

Sam, after our most recent battle I drew you a picture of one of the rebel cannons. Hopefully, that was the last we'll see of those.

Trina, we have seen snow in the air but not yet on the ground. Tell me about the snow in our yard. Is it up to the windows yet? Have you been sledding?

I pray God will continue to bless you in all your endeavors. As for us, we await God's will.

Your loving son and brother, Harm VanWyke

———

When Mother finished, she began to gather up the supper dishes.

When Sam and Trina offered to clean up, she didn't argue. She tousled Trina's hair and went to check on Father again.

As they cleaned the dishes, the two of them talked. "We went sledding today," said Trina.

"That sounds like fun."

"It was. But Bram de Groot got hurt."

"Kees' little brother? What happened?"

"He tried to stand up on the sled instead of sitting down."

Sam chuckled. "Of course he did."

"His mother said it was just a bump. She said he'll get better soon."

"That's good."

"Do you think Father will get better soon?"

Sam answered without hesitating. "Father will be all right. He's strong. And we need him."

## CHAPTER 37

# JANUARY 1865

At Cincinnati, the 25th Michigan left the steamers behind. They boarded rail cars and traveled on the B & O railway to Baltimore, then on to the nation's capital.

Washington was unlike any place they'd been. High-ranking officers strutted about town in uniforms which bristled with stars and stripes and ribbons and bows. At night, politicians, generals, and business titans gathered at lavish parties, bickering and bargaining as they ate and drank.

"Officers go to parties while soldiers survive on hardtack," scoffed Kees.

"Or don't survive," said Ted.

Harm thought of soldiers shivering in the cold, maybe bleeding on the battlefield, while the very important people in Washington went to parties. But he and his friends also lived well while they were in Washington. They slept in private apartments, enjoying the use of bath rooms, reading rooms, and more. They ate at tables.

Captain de Boe informed them they would likely stay in Washington until the ice on the Potomac broke up.

"Bath rooms are nice," said Ted.

"I hope we stay here for a while," said Willem. "This is where the important decisions are made. The war isn't won on the bat-tlefield. It's won here in Washington."

Harm wasn't impressed. "Maybe if the people here visited the battlefield once in a while, they'd find a way to end the war."

Soon after arriving in Washington, Spencer came to see Harm. "The local Philharmonic Society is giving a concert on Friday night."

"What's a Philharmonic Society?" asked Harm.

"An orchestra. They're playing Bach and Beethoven. Do you want to go?"

Harm jumped at the chance. He'd set aside some money for emergencies. An opportunity to hear an orchestra qualified. He invited his friends to join him.

"Sorry," said Kees. "Sounds boring."

Ted made snoring noises.

Gerrit still didn't think Harm should be spending time with Spencer.

"I'll go," said Willem.

On Friday night, Spencer, Clay, Harm, and Willem walked to Ford's theater on 10th Street. Harm surveyed the massive building in amazement. "It must hold a thousand people."

"Fifteen hundred," said Spencer.

The stage held two dozen chairs arranged in a semicircle around a conductor's podium. The musicians took the stage, tun-ing their instruments and warming up. Even that disorganized jumble sounded beautiful to Harm. He gazed up at the balcony. "Who gets to sit up there?"

"People with more money than you," said Spencer. He pointed to one of the private boxes. "President Lincoln attends concerts up there."

"President Lincoln is here?"

"Not tonight. But he does attend plays here."

The conductor took the stage and everyone fell silent. He moved his baton, and the orchestra began to play. Harm hardly breathed for the rest of the night. He lost track of time and all sense of place as the music transported him away.

The joyful, exuberant strains of Bach's Brandenburg Concerto No. 3 sent Harm's mind soaring. He thought of Sarah's embrace on the town square back in Holland—of her smile, the warmth of her body against his. He remembered the relief and joy he'd felt after the victory at Tebbs Bend on the Green River. The music seemed to capture all of the joy that King David must have felt when the Ark of the Covenant returned to Jerusalem.

Later, the orchestra played Beethoven's 7th symphony. Again, Harm was deeply affected. The piece began with a sweeping and beautiful melody, but the second movement took his breath away. With its somber, driving rhythm, it sent Harm's thoughts to the dark days after Howard's death, the misery he'd witnessed at Cassville and again in Atlanta. Ultimately, it brought to mind the sorrow Jesus experienced at the end of his earthly life, when even his friends forsook him.

The concert ended too soon. On the way back to camp, the four boys spoke excitedly about the power of music. Harm had always found solace in the psalms, simple yet profound. The scope and complexity of the orchestra only amplified that effect.

The next day, Spencer stopped to see Harm again. "So, you enjoyed the concert, then?"

"You know I did."

Spencer grinned. "Back in Atlanta, I wrote an old college professor about you. I told him I thought you could benefit from a Yale education. He just wrote me back. He agrees."

Harm laughed. "Did you tell him I'd have to pay for it in chickens?"

"Money isn't an issue. My father's a patron. He can pull some strings."

"You're joking."

"Not at all."

Harm's heart beat faster. He hadn't even allowed himself to dream of a college education. This seemed like a miracle, like a gift from God.

"Interested?" asked Spencer.

"Yeah. Maybe. I should discuss it with my parents."

"Of course. Let me know."

Spencer left, but Harm's heart continued to race. A college education. And not just any college. Yale. He could study anything he wanted: law or medicine, even music or literature.

The bugle announced mail call. Harm received two letters. The first was from his family. They thanked God he was safely in Washington. The weather back home was cold, and the snow was deep. The church planned to call a second minister as Rev. van Raalte could no longer do all the work himself. Trina had gone sledding with the girls in her class. Sam had taken Ella de Jong on a sleighride. Little Eliza had her second birthday. And Henry and Anna were expecting another child.

The second letter was from Sarah. She assured him she continued to pray for him. She kept his letters in a cherrywood box which Howard had built for her, and she followed his travels in her father's atlas. She included a poem she'd written about how spring holds its breath until the birds return from the South, because only when they are safely home can new life truly burst forth. It rhymed beautifully in the Dutch. She closed her letter with a prayer that Harm's father would soon be restored to health.

Harm read the line again. His father? He reread the letter from his family, wondering if he'd missed something, but they made no mention of his father being sick. Was Sarah confused? Or was his family hiding something from him?

He asked Willem about it. "Yeah, my father mentioned it. He said your father hasn't made it to church for a couple of weeks."

Harm felt a chill run down his spine. The last time he had seen his father, they had argued. He couldn't lose him, not now with the war almost over. He wrote home, demanding they tell him the truth.

All week he waited for their response. He found it hard to think of anything else. He even turned down an opportunity to attend a piano recital with Spencer. Finally, after ten days, he received a letter from home. Yes, his father had been sick—very sick, even. But he grew stronger every day. Sam was helping with the chores. Harm shouldn't worry.

Harm did worry. He went to ask Colonel Moore for an emergency leave of absence, but the colonel was away on business.

"Ask Major Harrod," said Willem.

Harm shook his head. "He doesn't like me."

"He doesn't like anyone," said Ted.

"He's a man who knows how to get things done," said Willem. "That's what matters. That's why I admire him. Go ask."

Harm was desperate. He went to see Major Harrod. "My father is sick. I need to get home."

"And I need a promotion," said the major without looking up from his work. "It seems both of us will be disappointed."

"But the war's almost over."

The major smirked. "I've been hearing that one for a year and a half now."

"We're stuck in Washington anyway. We can't head south until the ice melts."

"You'll have to do better than that. The weather in Washington changes like the president changes generals."

"I've got to get home," pleaded Harm. "My father is sick. He never gets sick."

Major Harrod paused as if reflecting. "If you truly need to get home, I can get you there."

Harm's heart soared.

"But first you have to do something for me."

"Of course. Anything."

"Win the war!" bellowed the major, slamming his fist down onto his desk.

Harm rose, stunned, and staggered back to his tent.

A week passed, and Harm received another letter from home. His family assured him his father made steady progress. He hoped to be back in church in a few weeks. Uncle Ben's letter to Willem also spoke of Harm's father's improvement. Harm began to breathe easier.

When Spencer invited him to another concert, he agreed to go. On Friday night, he joined Spencer, Clay, and Willem at a different theater. The crowd was larger than before, and younger. A large curtain hid the stage.

"It's a different kind of concert tonight," said Spencer. "More of a play."

"Shakespeare?"

"Not exactly. It's a comedy, with some musical numbers."

The curtain rose, revealing a forest of fake trees on one side and a table with chairs on the other. Music played, and a number of scantily clothed women took the stage. Harm looked at Spencer, then back at the stage. The women danced and sang. Harm averted his eyes, but their song proved as suggestive as their outfits. His face felt hot.

A group of men appeared from the far side of the stage and danced in amongst the women. The two groups traded barbs filled with bawdy innuendo. The audience loved it. They clapped and cheered. Spencer, too. Even Willem threw back his head in laughter.

The barbs continued, all in flowery language and rhyming couplets. The music perfectly matched the mocking lyrics. It was funny. But in that opening song, they'd managed to ridicule friendship, family, church, and government—all things God appointed as blessings for his people.

Harm had often marveled at the power of music to stir the soul. He suddenly realized it also had power to stir up the flesh.

Harm wanted to walk out. But what would Spencer think? Probably that he was too small-minded and narrow for a school like Yale. Spencer might even take back his offer. Harm felt frozen in place, like his whole future hung in the balance.

The song came to an end, and he breathed a sigh of relief. Perhaps he could get through the rest of the play. But the banter that followed was no better. Every line seemed designed to mock virtue and make sin seem funny or appealing. When one of the players took the Lord's name in vain, Harm's mind went back to the night he'd watched Kees play cards with Charlie Marley. The second time it happened, he excused himself and left the theater.

A blast of icy wind hit him at the door. He waited for Willem to join him, but he didn't come. He was about to head back to camp alone when Clay stepped out into the night. Harm looked at him in surprise.

"That play wasn't so good," said Clay.

"No," agreed Harm.

"It reminded me of what you said at devotions—about living

differently. I said to myself, 'If Harm enjoys the play, what he said before was just words.'"

Harm considered that. "Even when you know the right thing to do, sometimes it's hard to do it."

"I thought Willem would leave, too," said Clay.

Harm nodded. Willem had stayed for the same reasons Harm had stayed as long as he did. The music was exciting. The play was funny. And he didn't want to ruin his friendship with Spencer.

When Harm arrived back in camp, Gerrit approached him. "You're back early. How was the concert?"

"Not good," said Harm. He described what happened.

"Where's Willem?" asked Gerrit.

Harm didn't answer.

The next day, Harm tried to get Willem alone so they could talk about the play. But Willem spent the day helping Major Harrod with his paperwork.

That night at devotions, Gerrit read 1 John 2:15-17: *"Love not the world, neither the things that are in the world. If any man love the world, the love of the Father is not in him. For all that is in the world, the lust of the flesh, and the lust of the eyes, and the pride of life, is not of the Father, but is of the world. And the world passeth away, and the lust thereof: but he that doeth the will of God abideth for ever."*

Gerrit said, "We shouldn't love the things in the world. That includes its music."

Willem was ready for him. He replied, "Music is a gift from God. We should enjoy it."

"Not when it promotes the lust of the eyes and the pride of life," said Gerrit. "Which it will if the world makes it."

"Wait," said Kees. "Just because the world abuses something doesn't necessarily spoil it for us. Some people in the New Testament wouldn't eat food sacrificed to idols, but Paul said they should enjoy the good things of creation, even though the world misuses them."

"That's not the same," argued Gerrit.

"It's worse," said Kees. "They sacrificed it to *idols*."

"But the food itself was good," said Gerrit. "We should stick to good music. And we have that in the psalms."

"I love the psalms," said Harm. "But other songs can praise God, too. Think of those songs they sang that night at the Jemison's. Those were good, too."

"And that hymn we liked at that church at Nashville," said Ted.

"Even Bach and Beethoven," said Harm.

Gerrit shook his head. "That's going too far. You don't even know if Beethoven was a believer."

"Does it matter?" said Willem. "The world can do good things, too."

"No," said Gerrit. "They can't. Apart from Christ, all is sin."

Willem was on his feet and getting angry. "You wouldn't refuse to sail on a boat just because an unbeliever built it. Why should music be any different?"

"That's—," Gerrit started to object.

"Music *is* different," Harm interrupted. "A person's spiritual attitude shows itself in works of art. A believer makes different music than the world would."

"And yet you listen to Beethoven."

Harm hung his head. "I know. It's not so clear when a song doesn't have words. But that play . . . anyone could tell it was written to mock God's ways."

Willem looked sullen but said nothing.

Gerrit said, "If Beethoven wasn't a believer, his symphonies are no better than that play."

Harm considered that. "If Beethoven took God's gift and used it for his own glory, that's not good. Earthly pride doesn't please God. But his music can still help *us* praise God. When I listened to his symphony, it brought me to the foot of the cross. *That* pleases God, doesn't it?"

"You're making it too personal," argued Gerrit. "If it depends on us, how do we know what we should listen to and what we shouldn't?"

"I guess we have to make judgments," said Harm. "Every day about everything. We have to ask ourselves, does this please God or does it offend him?"

"We can't just *ask ourselves*," said Gerrit. "We'll always find an excuse for things we like. Our judgment has to be based on the Bible."

Harm realized Gerrit was right. Beautiful music would always appeal to his senses, even if its message was sinful. It would always present a temptation for him. He couldn't trust his own judgment. God's word was the only reliable measure.

"We underestimate the power of our sinful flesh," said Gerrit. "We think we can resist every temptation, but we can't."

Harm nodded. "That's why church is so important. The *dominie* can open God's word for us. We need the support of fellow believers." Harm looked at Willem as he spoke, but Willem refused to meet his gaze.

Harm wished he could find the right words to help his friend. He remembered Howard's phrase, *ora et labora*—pray and work. He prayed God would open Willem's eyes, and determined to speak to him again after devotions.

Later, when Harm brought it up, Willem said, "It was just a play. I don't know why everyone thinks it's so important. I just want Spencer to think we're normal, like everyone else."

"But we *are* different," said Harm.

"Yeah," sighed Willem. "I know." He sounded disappointed, like he wished it wasn't true.

## CHAPTER 38

# JANUARY – FEBRUARY 1865

In Virginia, General Grant and his Union forces lay siege to Petersburg. In Georgia, General Sherman prepared to drive north into the Carolinas. Meanwhile, the 25th Michigan remained in Washington, where a bitterly cold spell showed no signs of breaking.

Kees pulled his collar up around his neck. "I guess we'll be in Washington for a while."

"Good news, though," said Willem. "We're all invited to a party in Georgetown. I've been helping Major Harrod, and he said I can bring my friends."

"That's odd." Harm looked at the others. "Isn't that odd?"

Kees shrugged. "Who cares?"

"I'm not sure anything good happens at those parties," said Gerrit.

"Only one way to find out," Kees grinned. "I say we go."

Ted agreed.

The night of the party, Kees showed up with freshly-cut hair and a freshly-bathed body.

"Don't you smell pretty," said Ted.

Kees straightened his shirt. "Don't knock it till you've tried it."

Gerrit decided to stay behind. The others made their way to a luxurious mansion in Georgetown. A fresh layer of snow made everything shimmer in the lamplight.

Inside, the aroma of roast lamb and veal filled the air. Servants whisked trays of drinks to every corner of the house. Lively tunes mixed with laughter and the tinkling of glasses. Men in dark suits huddled together, discussing politics, business, and war strategy. Women swirled about in the latest fashions. The scent of perfume filled the air.

Kees made his way to the foot of a grand staircase, where two young ladies vied for his attention. Harm found his way to a small alcove off the main room where a string quartet played. Their bows swept gracefully across the strings. Harm lost himself in the music.

He turned when he heard Major Harrod's voice. The major had inserted himself into a group which included the secretary of the interior, where he proceeded to flatter the secretary and brag of his own accomplishments.

Willem and Ted joined Harm at the window. "Can you believe it?" said Willem. "I've met two generals, three majors, and a member of congress."

"I believe it," said Ted. "You can't turn around in here without stepping on a very important person."

After a few moments, Major Harrod joined them, reeking of whiskey. "Welcome, boys. Welcome." He nodded to Willem. "Good work."

"Thank you for inviting us," said Harm, trying to be polite despite a growing sense they shouldn't have come.

"Of course. Of course." The major gestured across the room. "Do you see that gentleman in the dark suit? He used to be the secretary of the war department."

"I hope that's his daughter on his arm," said Ted.

The major frowned. "You won't be joking when they put him in charge of reconstructing the South after the war. He's seriously considering me as his deputy. You could be my assistants. Are you listening? You could trade the mud and blood of the battlefield for the power and prestige of Washington. But you've got to play your cards right."

"I don't play cards anymore," said Ted.

Kees joined them, and Major Harrod addressed him. "I see you're a man of action. You could have a bright future in the war department."

"The war department?" said Kees. "What's the point? The war's almost over."

"*This* war," corrected the major. "War never really goes away."

Kees looked puzzled.

"You could go west, fight Indians."

"West?" Kees looked interested.

Harm turned away and walked to the far side of the room, where a large window looked out on a snow-laced garden below. He wished they'd stayed behind with Gerrit.

A few moments later, Major Harrod appeared at his side. He motioned in the direction of Kees. "He has a wild streak. I like that."

"I'm not like him," said Harm.

"No. You've got something else. The boys listen to you."

"What do you want?"

"This war is winding down, and that's a shame. But reconstruction is where the real money will be made. I aim to get filthy rich. Help me recruit your friends and I'll see you get a smudge on your fingers as well."

"No, thanks." Harm turned to go.

The major grabbed him by the shoulder and spun him around. "Don't be a fool. Your friend jumped at the chance."

Harm stared at him. "I told you, I'm not like him." He broke away and made his way to the door. Bursting outside, he drank in the cold, clean air. A thousand stars spanned the heavens. He spotted familiar constellations—Ursa Major and Orion—and wished he and his friends were back home again in Holland. He felt like everything was spinning out of control.

Eventually, Ted joined him outside, then Willem.

"What a night," said Willem.

Ted nodded. "I ate veal."

Harm didn't respond. The house was impressive, the food was delicious, and the music was beautiful. But as for Major Harrod's plans, he wanted no part in them.

Finally, Kees joined them, and they headed back to their rooms. Harm thought Kees would say something about Major Harrod's plans, but all he said was, "I need to write Susanna."

Later that week, Spencer stopped by and invited Harm and Willem to another concert.

"What kind of concert?" asked Harm.

Before Spencer could answer, Willem said, "Harm didn't like the last one."

Spencer looked at Harm. "Is that why you left? I thought maybe you were sick."

Harm's heart raced. He'd prepared himself to talk to Willem, but hadn't thought about what he might say to Spencer.

"I liked the music . . ." Harm began. He felt his whole future at Yale slipping away. All he had to do was close his mouth and everything would be all right. But Spencer was waiting for an answer. He sighed. "But to be honest, it went against everything I believe in."

Spencer looked surprised, then chuckled. "Well, that's honest."

"I thought it was funny," said Willem.

"It *was* funny," said Harm. "But that doesn't make it right."

Willem glared at him. "You sound like Gerrit. Don't act so 'holier-than-thou.'"

Harm cringed. He didn't want to be "holier-than-thou," but he *did* want to be holy. Wasn't there a difference?

Spencer waved the charge away with his hand. "It's all right. It's my fault. I should have realized."

Willem had no intention of being so gracious. "If you don't like the play, that's your problem, Harm, but don't get self-righteous about it."

Harm recoiled at the charge. He couldn't think of a worse accusation. He wasn't trying to say he was better than anyone else. He knew he was a sinner. He was only righteous because of Jesus.

"I know you're a religious person," said Spencer. "I respect that. But I get nervous when anybody tells me I have to do this or that to get into heaven."

"That's not what I'm saying," said Harm. "We can't earn anything with God."

"Then why not enjoy the play? What *are* you saying?"

Harm sighed. "God adopted me in Jesus. I want to live in a way that pleases him. That's not so strange. Children want to please their parents—not to avoid punishment, not to earn a place in their home, but just because they love them."

Spencer started to say something, then stopped. He grinned. "That's good, Harm. I've had this conversation with lots of people, and no one ever made that much sense."

"Come join our devotions again sometime," said Harm.

He shook his head. "I told you. I gave that up."

Harm hesitated, then looked Spencer in the eye. "I guess I won't be going to Yale."

"No?"

"I figured you'd change your mind after this."

"No way," said Spencer. "I think Yale is exactly what you need."

The next night, at devotions, Harm read from the book of Ezra, where Cyrus released Israel from captivity in Babylon and sent them back to Jerusalem to rebuild the temple.

"Ezra," said Kees. "Interesting."

"It has a good lesson for us," said Gerrit. "After seventy years in captivity, Israel had the opportunity to return to Jerusalem. But some chose to stay behind . . . in Babylon."

"You think that's what we'd be doing if we don't go back to Holland after the war?" asked Kees.

"Yes," said Gerrit.

Kees turned to Harm. "How about you?"

Harm considered the question. "Holland isn't the same as the promised land, no. But if we choose the things of this world over membership in a faithful church, that's still wrong."

"What matters is that we love God," said Willem. "As long as we have a good relationship with God, we shouldn't let the church stand in the way of doing what we want to in this world."

"But God teaches us how to live in this world," said Harm. "He teaches us to live in fellowship with his church."

After devotions, Harm tried to talk to Willem alone, but he stalked away.

## CHAPTER 39

# FEBRUARY 1865

The next day at mail call, Harm received three letters—one from his parents, one from his sister Anna, and one from Sarah. Then Captain de Boe held up another letter. "Ted? Ted Vogel?"

Ted wasn't there. He'd given up going to mail call way back in Louisville.

Harm offered to deliver the letter. He recognized the handwriting. Why would Rev. van Raalte write Ted? He found Ted and handed him the letter.

Ted looked at it, puzzled. He tore open the envelope and read the letter. His hand began to shake. He turned away.

"What's wrong?"

He handed the letter back to Harm. Rev. van Raalte did his best to lighten the blow, but he couldn't change the facts. Ted's father had drowned.

Harm looked up. "I'm so sorry."

"Yeah. Me, too."

Word of Mr. Vogel's death spread quickly through camp, and Ted's friends showed up to express their sympathies. Nearly everyone in the company had a good word for Ted. The fact that Mr.

Vogel had become somewhat notorious back home made condolences difficult, but still they came.

After the others had gone, Kees said, "We're your family now."

Harm agreed. "We're all children of God. That makes us brothers."

Ted thanked them and assured them he was all right, then slipped away to be alone.

Harm remembered Ted's father well. Mr. Vogel had managed to eke out a living on his farm, but seemed unable to sustain the effort necessary to improve it. More than once he began work on a barn, even gathering the wood necessary to build it. But after a day or two of hard work, he'd retreat to his house and stay inside for a week. He might have lost the farm a few times over the years if Harm's older brother, Jacob, hadn't helped him.

Memories flooded Harm's mind. He thought of Jacob, who had died in the springtime just months before Harm joined the infantry. Jacob had often helped Mr. Vogel bring in his harvest. He would rise early and put in two or three hours at the Vogel farm before returning to do his own chores at home.

Harm remembered waking before dawn to see him getting dressed.

"Why are you up so early?" he'd asked.

"I'm going to help Mr. Vogel," Jacob had said.

"But it's still dark."

"He's not feeling well."

"But it's your birthday."

Jacob had tussled Harm's hair. "You remembered."

"I made you a present."

"Go back to sleep. We'll celebrate tonight."

Harm had waited all day for him to return. His present had been a drawing of Father and Jacob working on their new house. He'd known Jacob would like it. He always liked his drawings.

At suppertime, Jacob still hadn't returned from the fields. Harm had begged his mother to let him stay up, but she'd sent him to bed. He'd left his drawing on Jacob's pillow.

When he awoke the next morning, Jacob had already left for Mr. Vogel's farm. But Harm's drawing was no longer on his pillow. He had nailed it up on the wall above his bed. In its place was a note: "*Thank you, Harm. This is your best drawing yet. I love the birds on the fence posts. I remember them singing while we worked.*"

Harm reflected on the memory. He wondered if his father had sent Jacob to help Mr. Vogel or whether he'd done it on his own. It would have been just like him to volunteer. He didn't wait around for people to ask for his help. His life was short, but he took every opportunity to help others.

Harm had resented Mr. Vogel back then. As he got older and got to know Mr. Vogel better, he realized his friend's father could be quite friendly, even lighthearted. But just as often, Harm caught the lost and vacant expression lurking just behind his eyes.

In mid-February, the weather in Washington turned warm and the ice on the Potomac began to break up. Colonel Moore announced that the 25th Michigan would leave Washington and join General Sherman in his efforts to drive the Confederate Army out of Wilmington, North Carolina.

"Finally," said Kees. "Back to the war."

Harm didn't share Kees' enthusiasm for fighting, but was glad to get out of Washington.

They boarded a twelve-hundred-ton steamer, *Matansas*, and steamed down the Potomac River toward the sea. On board the steamer, Captain de Boe announced mail call. He produced another letter addressed to Ted and asked Harm to deliver it. Harm stuffed the letter in his pocket without looking at it. He was tired of being the bearer of bad news. Finding Ted below deck, he delivered the letter.

Ted reached for the envelope but eyed it skeptically. "I'm not sure I can take any more news from home just now."

Harm returned above deck. He stood at the rail for a long time, watching the scenery change as they entered Chesapeake Bay. He pondered what the future held. Ted, it seemed, would go to Pella. Kees would probably go even further west. Who knew what Willem would do?

Once, Harm had feared his friends would go off to war and return with a thousand tales of adventure that didn't include him. Now, he feared he might be the only one to return to Holland. Him and Gerrit. Then it occurred to him, why should *he* return? He could go to Yale. His life could be larger than a forty-acre plot.

Later, Ted joined him on deck and handed him his letter. "It's a good letter. You should read it."

Harm recognized the handwriting. It was his father's.

———

*Holland, Michigan*
*February 1, 1865*

*Dear Ted,*

*I am so very sorry to hear of your father's passing. I know this comes as a shock. I will tell you what I know. He walked to town in a bitterly cold freezing rain. He ran into Mr. Koster and asked him if he had any news about you boys. He bought a newspaper and a bottle and turned toward home. The next day they found him in the stream just below the bridge, which was coated with ice. It appears he slipped on the bridge and fell into* the swollen stream where he drowned. We want you to know how very sorry we are.

I know you had a strained relationship, and it cannot be denied he failed to carry out his baptism vows. But in this time of loss, I urge you to remember also your godly mother. I knew her well, back in the Netherlands. We grew up in the same town and attended the same church. She and my sister were best friends and walked home from catechism together. She loved to skate on the canals in wintertime.

Later, when she heard we were going to America, she begged to go with us. She sincerely desired for you the opportunity to live and worship in freedom. Your father hesitated, fearing for her health, as she was often ill. But he agreed to go as he had trouble finding work. When she fell ill on the ship, he immediately regretted his decision. When she died, he was inconsolable.

In this time of grief, I encourage you to remember your dear mother. She willingly sacrificed home and country for your spiritual well-being. God took her to himself according to his perfect plan but her hopes for you can still be realized. Rev. van Raalte confirmed to me that your father held the deed to his land. That will now fall to you. Again, we express our sincere sorrow and pray that you may soon return and live the life your mother so dearly wanted for you.

Your brother in Christ,
H. van Wyke

---

"He's right," said Ted. "I was so young when my mother died, I never gave her much thought. Your father set me straight on that. She loved me."

Harm had never seen his father put that many words together at one time.

"He didn't have to do that," said Ted. "He didn't know how I'd react. But he cared enough to say something. I appreciate that."

"I'm glad it helped."

"He signed it 'Your brother in Christ,'" said Ted. "Just like we were talking about."

Ted returned below deck, but Harm remained at the rail. He was happy his father's words had cheered Ted. Sometimes, he wished he was more like his father.

The *Matansas* steamed out of Chesapeake Bay, past the boundary islands and entered the open ocean. It rolled from side to side as waves slapped its hull. Gulls cried overhead.

Kees called Harm on deck. "Look at this!" He pointed over the railing at the surface. A dozen porpoises were swimming alongside the boat.

Gerrit joined them at the rail. "We've seen so many things our parents never experienced."

"They saw the ocean, though," said Harm, "when they came to America." He breathed in the salty air, trying to imagine how his parents had felt when they left the Netherlands behind and sailed across the wide ocean in search of a new home. His parents weren't explorers by nature. Their lives revolved around home and church, farm and town. They left the Netherlands for one reason—so their children could live and worship in freedom.

Ted appeared on deck, and Kees waved him over. "How are you doing, Ted?"

"I'm all right," said Ted. "I thought the ocean might be hard. I thought it would remind me of my mother. And it does, but in a good way."

"How about you, Harm?" asked Kees. "Any word about your father?"

"My mother keeps telling me not to worry," said Harm, "but it's been a month, and he's still not back to church."

Kees nodded. "I've got bad news from home, too."

"What's that?"

"I got a letter from Johanna Meers. Remember her?"

"I remember you liked her."

"Yeah, well. She told me Melvin Moerdyke asked Susanna to go on a sleigh ride with him. And she went!"

Passion rose in Kees' voice and fire blazed in his eyes. Harm tried to tamp it down. "That doesn't mean anything, necessarily."

"Oh, it means something," snapped Kees. "It means he's a lousy schemer. If I was home, he wouldn't come within a mile of her. But no, I'm off saving the Union and he tries to steal my girlfriend."

"One of them," said Ted.

## CHAPTER 40

# FEBRUARY 1865

The 25th Michigan spent several days at sea as they made their way to North Carolina. Harm and his friends were together at the rail when they finally arrived at the mouth of the Cape Fear River. They passed a series of forts, culminating in Fort Fisher, guarding the way to Wilmington. The forts all flew Union colors.

"Looks like General Sherman won the war without us," said Gerrit.

"Those are just forts," said Kees. "He'll need us to take the city."

Willem joined them as they entered the river. He pointed to an odd-looking vessel patrolling the area. "That's one of those iron-clad monitors. I hoped to see one up close."

Harm admired how low it lay in the water, its one big turret rising above, ready to fire on Confederate blockade runners.

"Such a brilliant design," said Willem. "It would be almost impossible for a cannon to sink it."

Ted pointed out large dents in its turret. "Hasn't kept them from trying."

The steamer docked, and the 25th Michigan set up camp near other regiments which had arrived earlier. Harm noticed the flag of the 80th Indiana. Charlie Marley's regiment.

The next morning, Colonel Moore informed them the situation around Wilmington had changed dramatically. Union forces had taken the city just days earlier.

Kees was devastated. "The last big battle, and we missed it."

"Don't be so sure," said Captain de Boe. "They took the city. We still have to hold it."

Later, Charlie Marley stopped by. "*Now* you show up," he smirked. "After all the fighting is done."

Kees didn't want to talk about it, but Charlie was just getting started. "Where've you been? The last two weeks have been the most exciting of the whole war."

"And you were in the middle of it, I suppose," grumbled Kees.

Charlie grinned. "I hate to boast, but since you mention it, we saw a lot of action. We turned back a cavalry charge at Wilmington. That doesn't happen every day."

Kees tried to look bored.

"But the best part was Fort Fisher," continued Charlie.

Kees sighed. "You were there, too?"

"Fort Fisher was the key to the whole thing. Once the fort fell, we gained the river. The rebels had no way to resupply the city."

"And you took the fort single-handedly."

"Not at all. The Navy did most of the damage. But we got to their colors. I personally pulled the rope that lowered the Confederate flag. They might put me in the history books. I feel bad you missed it. Now it's too late."

"Don't be so sure," said Kees, echoing his captain. "You took Wilmington, but we still have to hold it."

"Sure," said Charlie with a smirk. "You can guard a railroad bridge or something."

Kees smoldered.

The next morning, Colonel Moore announced a return to drill

by company, regiment, and brigade. He was concerned a month in Washington had left the regiment unprepared for battle.

Kees went through the motions, but showed no spirit. Back at the tents, he said, "Why bother? The war's over."

"Don't count on it," said Willem.

Kees looked up. "You know something we don't?"

"Major Harrod says Colonel Moore wants to take Fort Anderson."

"What's Fort Anderson?"

"It's on the south bank of the river. It's the last rebel stronghold in the area."

"We already have the city," said Kees. "Why bother with another fort?"

"It's got a dozen big guns. That's probably where the dents in that monitor came from. Colonel Moore says we won't control the river until Fort Anderson is ours."

Kees cheered up considerably. The next day, he threw himself into drill with renewed energy.

One week after arriving in North Carolina, Colonel Moore announced a coordinated attack on Fort Anderson. The 25th Michigan marched out of camp at dusk, following the river. When they were well beyond the fort, they crossed over on flat-bottom barges and marched south. An hour later, they angled back toward the rear of the fort.

A waning moon gave little light as they skirted ponds and slogged through swampy bottomlands. Mud sucked at Harm's boots and coated his trousers.

Well after dark, Captain de Boe called them to a halt. "The fort is just ahead."

Harm peered into the night, but saw nothing. Kees pointed.

"There." The rebels had surrounded the fort with a series of low berm walls made out of sand, dirt, and stone.

"The monitor on the river will open fire on them," said the captain. "That should blast some holes in those berms. We'll hit them from behind. The 80th Indiana is on their flank. The rebels won't know where to turn."

Harm shivered in the darkness. He was wet past his knees. His hands felt slimy and cold. He wiped them on his coat, but they wouldn't come clean.

"Washington wasn't so bad," said Ted.

Kees grinned. "So much for the 'white glove regiment.'"

A moment later, the monitor on the river lit up the night with cannon fire. Harm watched in amazement as the cannonade smashed holes in the fort's defenses. Confederate skirmishers posted on the outer berms retreated in confusion as the bombardment destroyed their positions.

Colonel Moore signaled his troops to advance. Under cover of darkness, Harm marched forward through holes in the berm walls. Rebels fired blindly as they retreated, but did no damage. The flames erupting from their muskets served only to reveal their positions.

Harm and his friends reached the inner walls of the fort. "Follow me," said Kees. He leapt over a low wall and advanced toward a large parade ground.

Harm followed, unsure what Kees had in mind. Taking cover at the corner of a small building, Kees pointed across the parade ground. "That way."

Harm saw a raised platform. High above it flew a large Confederate flag.

"Let's go," shouted Kees.

"Wait," shouted Harm. "It's too open. It doesn't offer any cover."

"We can do it," insisted Kees. "We can't let Charlie beat us."

Harm stopped and stared at him. "What?"

Kees pointed at the Confederate flag. "I want those colors."

Before Harm could respond, Kees charged across the parade ground. Keeping low, Harm and the others followed. By the time they reached the platform, Kees was already at the flagpole, struggling with the ropes.

Harm pulled himself onto the platform. The parade ground was mostly empty. From the platform he could see over the walls of the fort to the moonlit river beyond. Out on the shimmering water, the dark silhouette of the monitor slid gracefully.

Suddenly, fire erupted from its cannon. On the far side of the parade ground, great mounds of dirt and stone exploded. Flames leapt into the night sky. Shadows raced about in confusion. Harm held his fire. In the darkness, he couldn't tell friend from foe.

Out on the water, the turret of the monitor swung a graceful arc in the moonlight. It stopped, pointing directly at the platform where Harm stood. Fire belched from its cannon.

"Take cover!" shouted Harm. But there was no cover. The ball struck just in front of the platform, showering it with rock and debris.

Gerrit staggered about in the darkness. "What happened?"

"It's the monitor," shouted Harm. "They must not realize we've advanced this far."

An explosion shook the platform, throwing Harm to his knees. He lost sight of his friends. Another shell exploded. The platform's timbers gave way, sending splinters and debris slashing through the air. Harm was knocked to the ground.

A cloud of choking dust enveloped the parade ground. Harm

scrambled away from the shelling. He looked for his regimental colors, but couldn't find them. Another explosion shook the fort. Someone shouted, "Fall back."

Harm saw shadows moving away from the fort and followed them. He stumbled, falling face down in the dirt. He rose to his feet, but was alone in the darkness. The sound of voices drew him through a gap in the berm walls and back into low brush and trees. Keeping to the brush, he moved toward the voices.

He recognized Kees' voice coming from a clearing and hurried to rejoin him. But Kees was on the ground, surrounded by Confederate soldiers.

Kees tried to warn him, but it was too late. Rebels leapt on Harm and drove him to his knees. They held him down and took his musket. More soldiers appeared, holding Ted and Gerrit.

A narrow-faced Confederate captain ordered them to their feet and lined them up.

"You don't want prisoners," said Kees. "We'll just slow you down."

"Silence," growled the captain.

"This war is over, anyway," said Kees.

The captain rammed the butt of his musket into Kees' belly, doubling him over. "You should have stayed home tonight." He pointed to a narrow path leading into the forest. "March."

Gerrit shot Kees a look. "Keep your mouth closed. Anything you say is just going to make it worse."

They marched in silence. Explosions and musket fire continued behind them, gradually fading into the night. Harm tried to remain calm. The soldiers had hard, hungry faces, but this was better than falling into the hands of bushwhackers. Soldiers, even rebel soldiers, had discipline. They followed orders. Harm and his friends might end up in a prison camp, but they wouldn't be shot and left for dead.

The soldiers led them south for an hour before stopping at a shallow creek to refill their canteens.

"How about us?" asked Kees, holding out his canteen. "Can we fill up, too?"

Gerrit glared at him.

The narrow-faced captain took Kees' canteen and filled it with water. Then he turned and strapped it over his own shoulder. The other soldiers laughed and began to follow his example.

Harm stood by helplessly as a greedy-looking private removed his canteen, haversack, cartridge belt, and ammunition. He sifted through Harm's rations, grinning as he stuffed them in with his own.

The soldiers resumed their march, eventually turning onto a cart path. The forest gradually thinned, revealing the shape of an occasional farmhouse in the moonlight. Soon, the group came to a halt at a small town that straddled a rail line.

Two old men in straw hats emerged from the train depot. "What's up, boys?"

"When's the next train?" asked the captain.

"A little over an hour," said one of the men. "If she comes at all. You know how it is these days."

The captain directed Harm and his friends up onto the platform.

"This is bad," said Gerrit.

Ted turned to Kees. "Maybe if you explain again why they should let us go . . ."

Kees didn't respond, but Harm could see in his eyes that a dozen potential escape plans were jostling for position.

The captain pulled two of his soldiers aside, an older lieutenant and a young private. "Put them on the next train," he ordered. "Escort them as far as Salisbury. Then meet up with us at Town Creek."

Before they could respond, he rejoined the other soldiers and they marched down the road.

The private, looking frightened, watched the other soldiers marching away. He called after the captain, "What if the train don't come?"

No answer.

He looked at the lieutenant. "What if the train don't come?"

"Never mind that," said the lieutenant. "What if the *Yankees* come?"

They looked at each other. An unspoken agreement had been reached.

Harm studied their faces in the dim light of the moon. They weren't killers, but they were frightened. Harm feared for his life. Here, with the war on its last breath, his candle might be extinguished. He shivered in the cold.

An hour passed, and the lieutenant began to pace impatiently. "I don't think it's coming."

Another twenty minutes, then he turned to the private. "That's long enough."

The private nodded nervously.

The lieutenant turned to the prisoners. "Come down off that platform."

Gerrit groaned and moved toward the steps.

Harm's heart thundered.

Kees showed no signs of fear. In fact, he became talkative. "What unit are you boys with, anyway?"

They ignored him.

"I'd just like to know who got the best of us," continued Kees.

Gerrit stopped and stared at Kees in disbelief, but the young private answered, "We're with the 21st South Carolina."

"*South* Carolina?" said Kees. "How long you been away from home?"

The young guard looked nervously at his lieutenant and said nothing.

"Are you with General Braxton Bragg then?" said Kees.

No answer.

"Now *there's* a general," Kees spoke with admiration. "We first heard his name back in Kentucky in '62. He whipped our General Buell at Perryville."

"He whipped your General Rosecrans, too," said the lieutenant, "at Chickamauga Creek."

"So I heard," said Kees. We were busy elsewhere. Where else you boys been?"

"We were at Cold Harbor."

"How'd that go?"

"We whipped your General Grant," said the lieutenant. "Seems there isn't a Union general we haven't whipped."

They kept on then, telling stories of daring deeds and bold victories, until a train whistle pierced the night.

The lieutenant stopped. "Well, there it is. About time."

"Where we headed?" asked Kees.

No answer.

"Kalamazoo?" offered Ted.

"Salisbury," said the lieutenant.

"Never heard of it," said Kees.

"Prison camp. You must be new around here."

"We shipped in a week ago."

"That so? Hope you ate well. They don't at Salisbury."

The train pulled up to the station with a rattle and a sigh. The lieutenant looked it over and spoke with the conductor. When he returned, he directed the prisoners to a rickety car near the back of the train.

They entered the old converted cattle car and the door slammed closed behind them. A padlock clicked into place. The car had no windows and no benches. It was dark, except for wedges of light that angled in through the slats.

They put their faces to a gap in the slats. The lieutenant instructed the private to sit on the back of the train and keep watch. "If they try to escape, don't hesitate to fire on them."

A few moments later, the train jerked and the cars rolled forward.

Kees stalked about the car in frustration. "I say we bust out."

"What about the guard?" asked Gerrit.

"I don't care," said Kees. "I'm not closing out this war in a prison camp."

Harm couldn't see much in the dark, but he worked his way around the car, feeling for loose boards. Near the back, he found a section that was warped and rotten. He showed Kees, who kicked at the boards, opening up a ten-inch gap. Air rushed in. He kicked again, widening the gap.

Harm knelt down and peered out. The ground underneath rushed past in a blur of black and gray. The roar of the wheels made him sick.

"What do you think?" asked Kees.

Harm shook his head. "The fall would kill us."

"A prison camp will kill us, too."

"Any options that don't kill us?" asked Ted.

"Better to die in a bold escape than rot in a prison camp," said Kees. "Where's the glory in that?"

"Never mind glory," said Gerrit. "How about getting home alive?"

"Jumping is still our best chance," said Kees.

Harm said, "I won't stand in your way if *you* want to go."

Kees shook his head. "I'm not leaving anyone behind. It's all or none."

"So, that's settled then," said Ted.

"Come on," said Kees. "A quick fall and we're free."

Harm knelt again, staring out at the blackness. "We could be over a trestle bridge. We could fall a thousand feet."

Kees sighed. "All right. You win. We rot in a prison camp."

Five minutes passed. Then the train began to shudder and shake. The floor tilted beneath them. The roar of the wheels on the rails diminished to a hum.

"What's this?" asked Gerrit.

"An upgrade," said Kees. "A steep one."

Harm moved to the gap in the boards and peered out. He couldn't make anything out in the darkness, but the churning of the wheels had slowed dramatically.

"What do you think?" asked Kees.

Harm kicked out another board. "It's now or never."

Ted nodded. Harm dropped to a knee and hurled himself into the darkness.

## CHAPTER 41

# FEBRUARY 1865

Formless gray clouds hung low over the van Wyke home, deepening as evening approached. A heavy silence hung over the home as it had since the arrival of the telegram announcing that Harm and his friends were missing and likely captured by the enemy.

Father had mostly recovered from his sickness, but the news of Harm's capture set him back. He sent Sam to town to do his errands.

Mother busied herself, sweeping out the entryway again, but couldn't conceal her worries. Trina helped without being asked.

In town, the postmaster handed Sam an envelope addressed to his parents. Sam didn't recognize the handwriting. Their name was misspelled. He tore open the envelope and read it right there in the post office.

Sam returned home, stopping at the door to regain his composure before entering the house. The family gathered, hoping for good news and dreading the worst. Sam read the letter.

———

Wilmington North Carolina
February 24, 1865

Dear Mr. and Mrs. VanWike,

Hello. You don't know me but I am a drummer in the army and I know Harm pretty well and I sure hope he is all right. He tells me stories about Sam and Trina which I like to hear because I don't have a brother or a sister or even a father or mother. He tells me about your church too and your minister, VanRowlty. I didn't believe in God because why would he make my parents die, but Harm believes in God even though he made his brother die so maybe I believe in God too. Harm tells me about Adam and Eve and about Jesus and lots of other stories from the Bible. I especially like Daniel and Joseph and Ruth. If I had a teacher like him, I would have stayed in school instead of joining the army. So mostly I want you to know that Harm has been a friend to me and I am sorry that he is missing and if he got captured, I hope he gets away.

Clayton Ernest Fowler

---

In the few minutes it took to read the letter, full darkness settled over the farm. Father's face looked gray as he rose from the chair and made his way back to his bed. Sam went out to the barn to complete his chores. Trina wiped down the table and washed the dishes.

Mother sat alone by the fire, her head bowed, clutching Harm's portrait to her breast.

## CHAPTER 42

# FEBRUARY 1865

Harm hit the ground headfirst, tumbled, and came to rest in a tangle of bushes. The train continued up a steep rise and disappeared around a bend. Harm rose to his feet and brushed himself off. He'd scraped his head and bruised a shoulder, but nothing seemed broken. He stood in the moonlight, breathing in fresh clean air of freedom.

A cloud blotted out the moon and Harm realized he stood alone, unarmed, in rebel territory. He moved deeper into the brush.

Several minutes later, footsteps approached in the darkness. Harm's heart pounded in his chest.

"Harm," a voice hissed. "Where are you?"

Harm recognized Kees' voice and stepped forward. Kees approached, followed by Ted and Gerrit.

"There you are," said Kees. "What a relief. We need to keep moving. When they realize we're gone, they'll come looking for us."

The four of them followed the rails back the way they'd come. At first, they talked excitedly, but as the night wore on, they walked in silence.

After an hour, Kees stopped, raising a hand to halt the others. Dark silhouettes of buildings rose up ahead.

Harm recognized the buildings. "It's the town where we boarded the train."

"We should have a look around," said Kees. "Maybe we can get our gear back."

Harm shook his head. "Those soldiers took our gear with them."

"How about a drink, then?" said Kees. "Those old boys at the depot probably keep a barrel of cider."

"We're unarmed," said Harm. "We can drink all we want when we get back to camp."

Kees agreed reluctantly. They left the rails, skirted the town, then circled back to the tracks.

The eastern sky began to lighten. They left the rails again and found a patch of forest where they could hide. A creek wound through the wood and they all stooped to drink. Gerrit sighed with pleasure at the cold, clear water. "Who needs cider?"

Harm knew what he meant. It was the best water he'd ever tasted.

"Go ahead and sleep," said Kees. "I'll keep the first watch."

Harm sat on a flat rock, his stomach growling with hunger. Out of habit, he reached for his haversack. It wasn't there.

Ted chuckled. "Hardtack never sounded so good."

Harm slept then, but woke again by noon, even hungrier than before. They explored the forest looking for food, but they saw no game, and it was too early for berries.

A small farm bordered the wood on one side. "We could take a look inside that barn," said Kees.

Harm was tempted, but the farmer and a nearly grown boy stood in the yard, splitting wood.

"We could jump them," suggested Kees. "It's four against two. And they're unarmed."

"What do you call those axes?" said Ted.

Gerrit crouched in the shadows. "They might have weapons nearby. One old musket would outgun us."

"A pitchfork would outgun us," said Ted.

Kees agreed. "Maybe they have a corn crib around back."

Before they could check, a couple of dogs yapped at each other somewhere behind the barn. Harm and his friends quickly withdrew into the deeper forest.

Once more they settled into hiding. Harm managed to nap again, but woke late in the afternoon. His nerves began to fray as the hours dragged on. Once, a twig snapped and he spun around, expecting to face Confederate soldiers. He jumped every time a dog barked.

When color began to drain from the sky, Kees suggested they move on.

"Not yet," said Harm. "It'll be dark soon."

"Maybe the attack on the fort was successful," said Kees. "Maybe we pushed the rebels out of the area."

"Maybe," agreed Harm. "but we still have to think about bushwhackers." They all remembered what had happened to Otto Boot.

Dusk gave way to full dark, and they took to the rails again. The night was still, with no moonlight and no breeze. Harm expected to reach the river at any moment. But they marched all night and still no river. As morning approached, a deep rumble sounded in the west.

"Cannons?" asked Gerrit.

Kees shook his head. "Thunder."

It rumbled again, louder and longer.

They picked up their pace as forks of lightning flashed in the west.

Finally, they came to the river. A trestle bridge stretched across the water to a town on the other side. It wasn't yet dawn, and the streets appeared empty.

"What do you think?" asked Kees. "Shall we cross over?"

Wind swept through the streets, heavy with the scent of rain. Lightning split the sky.

Harm nodded. "Hopefully the storm will keep folks inside."

They slipped from the brush and raced across the bridge. Harm crouched as he ran, keeping as low as possible. He was breathing heavily when he reached the far side of the bridge. The main street of the town was dark, but some of the houses had lights coming from their windows. They reached a cross street and turned toward Wilmington.

Suddenly, a large black dog appeared in the street, growling at them.

"Shhh," said Kees. "It's all right, Koffie. We're all friends here."

Koffie was the name of the de Groot's little terrier. This was no terrier.

They continued down the street, hoping he would lose interest. He didn't. He snarled and began barking.

A light went on in a shop. A man opened a door, peering out at them. "What are you folks up to?"

They stood deep enough in the shadows that Harm was confident the man wouldn't recognize their uniforms.

"I asked you a question." He walked toward them. "What's going on here?"

Kees cleared his throat.

"Don't answer," hissed Harm. "Keep moving."

Kees ignored him. "We're just lookin' for a friend of ar'n. But we're fixin' to move on, I reckon. Y'all needn't worry now."

Harm hung his head. When Kees broke out his southern accent, things rarely ended well.

The man stepped up to the door of a nearby barber shop and banged on the door. "Jesse, Tom, get out here."

Kees didn't wait for Jesse and Tom. He bolted around the corner with Harm and the others at his heels. They jumped a hedge, cut through a neighboring yard, and fled down a narrow alley.

The dog barked and the men shouted. Kees didn't stop until they'd reached the edge of town.

Ted caught up, huffing and puffing. "We need someplace to . . . hide . . . and rest."

Kees pointed toward a church building, dark against the gray sky.

"We can't hide in a church," said Gerrit. "People *go* to church."

"Not on a Friday morning," said Kees. They slipped through the shadows and Kees tried the door. It was locked. He examined the lock. "It's old. I can bust in if there are no objections."

Huge drops of rain began to fall, splatting on their caps and shoulders. The dog barked again, closer than before. There were no objections.

Kees put his shoulder to the door and it burst open. Once they were inside, the rain came in torrents. It roared on the church's slate roof.

Kees checked for other exits in case they had to leave in a hurry. Harm stood at the window, watching for pursuers.

"Anything?" asked Gerrit.

Harm scanned the gray morning but saw nothing. Still, it was several minutes before his breathing returned to normal.

"This is no poor country church," said Kees, walking about the spacious interior. "Look at this woodwork."

Ted tested the benches. "A bit hard for sleeping, though."

"Look at the carving on this table," said Harm. "This is a work of art."

"Hard benches in a finely appointed church building," said Ted.

Harm wasn't sure he could sleep anyway. What if there was a wedding or a funeral? They could be discovered at any moment.

"I'm starving," said Kees. "We should check out the parsonage. A church with a gold-plated baptismal isn't going to leave their pastor with an empty pantry."

Gerrit shook his head. "We're not doing that."

Kees gazed across the yard at the parsonage. "It's pretty dark over there. I'll bet the *dominie* left town until the fighting's over."

"It's not right," said Gerrit.

"Maybe," said Kees, "but if the minister was home don't you think he'd offer us something to eat?"

Gerrit didn't answer.

"What would Rev. van Raalte do if he came across four starving rebels? He wouldn't deny them a meal and a bed."

Ted rose wearily. "A bed sounds nice."

"It'll be safer," said Kees. "It's got a better view of the lane."

"It's closer to the forest, too," agreed Harm. "In case we have to escape in a hurry."

They dashed through the rain to the house. One broken door handle later, they entered the parsonage. A quick search confirmed it was empty. Harm sank into a deep, cushioned chair with a view of the lane.

"Look at this place," said Kees. Large portraits graced the parlor. The windows were framed with lace curtains. A grandfather clock stood in the hall.

Kees disappeared into the cellar and returned with a side of bacon and a jar of peaches. Harm hadn't eaten in two days. He accepted a slab of the salt pork.

"I'm not stealing from a church," said Gerrit, refusing to eat. He wandered off to explore the rest of the house.

Ted sighed as peach juice dribbled down his chin. "It's war."

"We should get some sleep," said Kees. "Tonight, we'll take the road back to Wilmington and find our camp."

A few minutes later, Gerrit reappeared. "I have to show you something."

They followed him to a room lined on three sides with bookshelves. "It's the minister's library. He's a Presbyterian, but look— Luther. Calvin. Bullinger."

Kees raised an eyebrow. "Bullinger?"

Harm chuckled. "He's one of the good ones."

"These are in Latin," said Gerrit, pointing to a row of very old books.

Harm eyed a beautiful leather-bound volume. *The Institutes of the Christian Religion*, by John Calvin."

Gerrit held up a red leather copy of a Greek New Testament.

Ted leafed through a Bible with ornate lettering colored in red and blue and green. "Does Rev. van Raalte have books like these?"

"His aren't this fine," said Gerrit. "These are treasures."

Kees yawned, "Who wants to take the first watch?"

"I'll stay up," said Gerrit.

"All right. Wake me at noon. I'll take the second watch." Kees disappeared in search of a bed.

Harm found some blank paper to write a note to the minister. He wanted to pay for the food they'd eaten, but the Confederate soldiers had taken his money. He wrote a note anyway, explaining about the food and asking forgiveness. With his conscience somewhat eased, he found a bed. He thanked God for watching over him and his friends, and prayed he would guide them back to camp.

When Harm awoke, the sun no longer shone in the window. Judging by the shadows, it was early evening. He hadn't intended to sleep that long or that deeply. Sounds came from inside the house. Had the minister returned? He slipped out of the bed and crept back toward the dining room.

Ted sat by the window, reading an old newspaper and eating another portion of bacon.

Kees sat at the table, laboring with pen and ink. "Harm, how'd you sleep?"

"Pretty well," said Harm. "What are you working on?"

"I found some paper in the cupboard," said Kees. "I've been writing a letter to Susanna."

"Good for you."

Kees folded the letter and inserted it into an envelope. He picked up a set of decorative hair combs. They were fancy, carved from whale bone and inlaid with precious stones. He dropped them into the envelope as well.

"What are those?" asked Harm.

"Just a little something to make Susanna forget about Melvin Moerdyke."

"Where'd you get them?"

"Upstairs. They're not expensive."

"They look expensive," said Ted.

"And they're not yours," said Harm.

Fire leapt into Kees' eyes. "Don't fight me on this, Harm."

Harm scanned the room, looking for Gerrit, but he was nowhere to be seen. Probably back in the library admiring the minister's books.

"Let it go," said Kees.

Harm sighed. He'd let too many things go. He'd made excuses for his friends and excuses for himself and it wasn't right. He'd let Gerrit take the heat for pointing out the difference between right and wrong. Well, Gerrit wasn't here this time.

He stepped between Kees and the doorway. "Leave the combs here."

Kees stepped closer to Harm, his eyes ablaze. "You going to make me?"

"If I have to."

"I don't want to hurt you, Harm."

"You'll have to."

Kees looked suddenly beaten. "Don't you get it? Melvin's home and I'm not. I'm losing her."

"They went on a sleigh ride. So what? You haven't written her in six months. Now you're all broken up?"

"That was wrong. I've been selfish. That's why I *need* to make it up to her."

"Not like this," said Harm. "We've taken food when we had none and boots when we needed them, but we're not taking hair combs to impress a girl. Don't tell me war makes *that* right."

"I'm going through that door," said Kees.

Harm looked into his darkening eyes. Someday, Kees would realize taking the combs was wrong. But Harm couldn't wait for that day. He had to stand up for what was right now. Even if Kees hated him for it. He said, "Not with those combs."

Kees started to turn away, then swung shoulder-first into Harm's chest. Harm lost his hold on the door and stumbled backwards. They fell through the doorway and into the yard.

They rolled as they hit the ground, and Harm ended up on top of Kees. He tried to pin him to the ground, but Kees wrenched himself free. He scrambled to his feet and lunged at Harm. They both fell into a stand of laurel bushes.

Kees dragged Harm out and wrestled him to the ground. Harm managed to spin free and stagger to his feet, but before he could throw a punch, Kees hit him with a blow that split his cheek open below his left eye. Blood streamed down his face.

Kees stepped back, and Ted jumped between them. Kees leaned against the house to steady himself. He looked at Harm and slumped to the ground. "Get him a towel or something."

Ted found a towel to wipe the blood from Harm's face, but Harm pushed it away. "This isn't over yet."

"Take the towel," said Kees. "You win." He went back inside the house and slammed the combs down on the table. When he returned, he said, "But if Susanna marries Melvin Moerdyke, I'm going to marry your Sarah and see how *you* like it."

## CHAPTER 43

# FEBRUARY 1865

Under cover of darkness, Harm and the others left the parsonage and made their way through the forest until they came to the road to Wilmington. Harm expected Gerrit to confront Kees about the combs, but he didn't. Gerrit hadn't eaten in twenty-four hours, so maybe that was it.

They trudged for an hour in sullen silence. The night was clear, and the moon had not yet risen. Suddenly, a shooting star sliced through the sky. Kees' eyes flew wide. "Harm! Did you see that? Just like that time on your birthday. Remember?"

Harm remembered. He, Kees, Ted, and Gerrit had built a raft and paddled out onto Lake Michigan. In maybe an hour, they'd counted over fifty shooting stars.

"How old were we?" asked Kees. "Twelve?"

Harm nodded. "The first time. Then we went out the next year, but it stormed."

"That's right," said Gerrit. "We barely made it back to shore."

Kees grinned. "Yeah, that was great. We'll have to do that again when we get back home."

The others agreed. The incident at the parsonage was all but forgotten.

"How far is it back to camp?" asked Gerrit.

Kees shrugged. "Don't know."

"Do you think we'll be there by morning?"

"Don't know."

"But other than that, we should be fine," said Ted.

An hour later, Kees stopped abruptly. He motioned the others to get down. He took a few steps forward and stopped again.

"What is it?" hissed Gerrit.

"Someone's out there."

"Who?"

"I intend to find out." He picked up a stone and threw it off to their left.

It struck high in a tree, cluttering from branch to branch as it fell to the ground.

A voice rang out. "Halt. Who's out there?"

Harm recognized the voice.

"Rinze?" shouted Kees. "Is that you? It's Kees."

The trees rustled and several Union pickets emerged. One of them was Rinze Rietema. "Are you all right? We thought you were captured."

"We were," said Kees. "We escaped."

More pickets appeared, all asking questions. "Come with me," said Rinze. "We've got to get you back to camp."

Captain de Boe questioned them and congratulated them on their escape. He arranged for something to eat and sent them to their tents.

When they awoke, Colonel Moore summoned them to his tent. He questioned them on every aspect of their capture, imprisonment, escape, and return. Kees answered most of the questions and kept mostly to the facts.

"Did they mistreat you?" asked the colonel.

"They took our gear," said Kees. "Weapons, too."

The colonel looked at Harm. "How'd your face get beat up, son?"

Harm raised a hand to his bruised cheek and stammered. "That was . . . um . . . unrelated."

The colonel raised an eyebrow, but didn't pursue it. Instead he turned to the attack on Fort Anderson. "In the confusion, the monitor opened fire on a portion of the fort we'd already taken. I presume that's what led to your capture. But the fort is ours, along with complete control of the river. And with no casualties, now that you're accounted for."

The colonel commended them for their bravery and sent them to the quartermaster to draw new weapons and gear.

Word of their return spread rapidly through camp. That evening, waves of soldiers appeared at their campfire, all wanting to hear their story. Kees was happy to oblige.

With each retelling, they became bolder, braver, and more heroic. Harm had to smile when Kees told of insulting General Bragg to the rebels' faces. He snorted with laughter when Kees told of fooling the townsfolk with his expert southern accent.

Charlie Marley stopped by to hear the story. At one point, he sighed and said, "I wish I'd been there."

Kees beamed with joy.

Gerrit was the only one who didn't seem to enjoy the celebration. He soon shuffled back to his tent.

"What's wrong with *him*?" asked Harm.

"He's probably still angry at me for making him jump off that train," said Kees. "Or breaking into that church."

"Or breaking into the parsonage," said Ted. "There's plenty of reasons to choose from."

Later, Frank de Windt came around, looking for trouble. He

told Kees, "Don't bother writing Susanna about your escape. I already wrote Melvin Moerdyke so she's sure to hear about it."

Kees pretended to ignore him, but Harm could tell the blow had stung. First, Kees grew unnaturally quiet. Then he slipped away from the fire altogether. When he hadn't returned after an hour, Harm went to his tent to check on him. He wasn't there.

Harm returned to the fire and motioned for Ted to join him. "I'm worried about Kees."

"What else is new?"

"I know, but I can't find him."

"Did you check with Charlie Marley?"

They walked over to the camp of the 80th Indiana. They didn't find Charlie, but they found one of his friends. "He was here earlier," said the soldier. "I don't know where he is now."

"Was he with anyone?" asked Harm.

"Yeah. He was with Bill and your friend, Kees."

"Kees was here?"

"He was all worked up about some girl. Charlie said he knew how to win a girl's heart. Something about combs."

Harm's heart sank.

"What should we do?" asked Ted.

Harm thought about telling Captain de Boe, but worried Kees would end up in the stockade for good. "We'll have to go after them."

Ted nodded. "Get Gerrit. Willem, too."

Harm found Gerrit in his tent and told him about Kees. Gerrit lowered his eyes. "You don't need my help."

"I know you don't approve of everything he does," said Harm. "I don't either. But he's still our friend."

Gerrit turned away. "You don't want my help."

Ted was impatient to get started. "Come on, Harm. We have to go."

Willem's tent was empty, but they found him with the quartermaster, taking inventory. Harm explained about Kees.

"Leave me out of it," said Willem. He didn't even look up from his ledger book.

"Kees might be in trouble."

"He's always in trouble."

"He's our friend."

Willem shook his head. "I've got my future to think of. I can't let Kees drag me down. You shouldn't either."

"Come on," said Ted. "Let's go."

They each had a brand new musket, but Harm wished they were better armed. He remembered Kees' pistol and decided to check his tent. He found the breastplate Kees had bought way back in Kalamazoo, and the belt plate with the letters CSA, which he'd taken from a Confederate soldier after the battle at Tebbs Bend—but no pistol.

Ten minutes later, Harm and Ted slipped past the pickets and retraced their steps from the previous night. Harm was hopeful they'd soon run into Kees and Charlie and Bill returning to camp. But the further they went, the more he worried.

After a couple of hours on the road, they stopped at the edge of the forest which lay behind the parsonage. "Listen," hissed Ted.

Harm heard branches snapping and heavy footsteps. Two shadows crashed through the trees directly in front of them. In the moonlight, Harm saw Charlie Marley.

"Charlie!"

Charlie stopped. With a trembling voice he said, "Who's there?"

Harm stepped into the moonlight. He saw Charlie and Bill, but no Kees. "It's me, Harm."

Charlie edged forward, obviously relieved.

"Where's Kees?"

"Kees is gone."

"What do you mean, gone?"

"Bushwhackers got him."

"Where? When?"

"Just a minute ago." He waved an arm back toward the parsonage.

"How many?" asked Harm.

"At least four."

"We've got to go back and help him."

Charlie's eyes flashed yellow in the moonlight. "You can do what you want. We're heading back to camp."

"Without Kees?!"

Charlie grabbed hold of Harm's collar and shook him. "Bill and I were never here. Understand? You never saw us." Then they were off again, crashing away through the woods.

Harm and Ted crept closer to the parsonage, trying to make no sound. The house was dark, but pricks of light swayed back and forth in the trees.

"Lanterns," hissed Harm.

"Maybe the minister came back," whispered Ted.

They crept closer, keeping to the shadows. In the lantern light, Harm saw shapes moving. A horse whinnied.

Harm dropped to his belly and pulled himself forward with his elbows. He found cover behind a giant stump. Kees was surrounded by three men. None wore uniforms.

A hard-faced man with massive forearms stood over Kees. He kicked him behind the knees, driving him to the ground.

"That's no minister," whispered Ted.

Harm agreed. Together, they worked out a plan. It wasn't much. They'd get as close as possible and then leap into the clearing with guns blazing. Hopefully the element of surprise would give them an edge.

Harm crawled forward and strained to get a better look. A heavy man with a pork pie hat knocked Kees' cap off, laughing as he stomped it in the dirt.

The tallest of the men, maybe the leader, said, "That's enough, Earl. Take off his jacket."

"Aw, Joe, I'm just havin' some fun." Earl stripped Kees' coat from him.

The one called Joe said, "Why you snoopin' around Rev. Graham's place?"

Kees didn't answer.

Earl rifled through Kees' pockets. He pulled out a letter and the combs. "Look here, Joe. Looks like he's got himself a gal."

"What's the letter say?" asked Joe.

Earl fumbled to open it. "It don't say nothin'. Just a bunch of scrapin'."

"That's 'cause you cain't read," said a fourth man, hidden in the shadows.

"Enough talk," said Joe. "You know what to do with him."

The hard-faced man pulled Kees to his feet and prepared to lead him from the clearing.

Ted nudged Harm. Together, they burst out of the shadows. The bushwhackers turned and gaped in disbelief. Earl brought his musket up, but Harm fired first. Ted fired next, and Joe fell. The hard-faced man pushed Kees to the ground. The fourth man bolted for the horses.

Harm reloaded as quickly as he could.

The hard-faced man leveled his musket at Harm, but Kees lunged at him from behind, knocking him to the ground. The fourth man reached the horses and managed to get into the saddle. He fired his musket across his body as he fled the clearing.

Kees cried out, grabbing his arm.

The hard-faced man lurched to his feet. He raised his musket and trained it on Harm's chest. Smoke and flame billowed out from his weapon.

Harm felt the ball strike him square in the chest and fell backwards. Somewhere, another musket fired.

"Harm!" cried Kees, scrambling to his side. He pulled at Harm's coat but couldn't open it with his good arm. "You all right, Harm? Tell me you're all right." He turned to Ted. "Help me with his coat."

Ted pulled Harm's coat open and gasped.

Harm opened his mouth, but no words came out. He couldn't seem to focus. Everything began to spin. Then all went dark.

## CHAPTER 44

# FEBRUARY – APRIL 1865

Harm awoke to darkness. Where was he? Was he dead? He tried to sit up, but sharp knives of pain stabbed at his chest. Not dead, then. He sensed others in the room and managed to turn his head. A row of beds lined a drab gray wall. A hospital.

Later, he awoke again. This time, the room was dimly lit. Early morning, he guessed. A surgeon stood nearby, fussing over another patient. Harm tried to speak, but no sound came out. The surgeon completed his task and moved away.

The next time Harm awoke, the sun shone brightly. Ted stood at his side. "Welcome back. They told me you were coming around."

Harm felt groggy. "Where am I?"

"The hospital in Wilmington."

"What happened?"

"You don't remember? Bushwhackers."

Harm tried to piece things together.

"We went looking for Kees at the parsonage."

Suddenly, the memories came crashing back. Harm put a hand to his chest. "I should be dead."

"You're full of surprises."

Harm replayed the scene in his mind. The narrow-faced bush-whacker fired at him. The ball struck him in the chest. Why wasn't he dead?

Then he remembered Kees' breastplate. "It worked?"

"All around you boys was fallin'."

Harm laughed, but fresh stabs of pain left him gasping for breath.

Ted held up the brass plate for him to see. A deep dent marked the spot where the ball struck it. A jagged scar ran from there to the edge, where the ball had skidded off.

"It saved your life," said Ted, "but left your chest three shades of purple."

"It hurts when I move."

"With hints of yellow, green, and orange."

Harm held up a hand to make him stop.

"What made you put that thing on, anyway?"

"I spotted it when I checked for his pistol. I thought we might meet up with trouble."

"That we did."

"What happened after I fell?"

Ted filled him in. "Kees was hit in the arm. But he wouldn't let me look at him. He just kept trying to wake you up. He was a slobbering mess."

"How'd you get us back to camp?"

Ted smiled. "I was trying to decide which one of you I was going to carry on my back when the patrol showed up. You had a slight lead."

"What patrol?"

"After we left, Willem told Major Harrod about Kees being absent without leave. The major sent out a patrol to arrest him."

"I can't believe Willem would do that."

"I'm glad he did. I couldn't have gotten you back to camp on my own."

"What about Charlie and Bill?"

"They must be laying low. I haven't seen them around."

"And Kees?"

"He's here in the hospital, just down the hall."

"Is he all right?"

"He's alive. They had to take his left arm at the elbow."

Harm groaned. He'd seen soldiers with amputations, but couldn't picture Kees that way. He tried to sit up, but the room began to spin.

A week passed before they let Harm out of bed. Then a nurse helped him travel as far as Kees' ward.

Kees was playing cards with another patient. When he saw Harm, he dropped the cards in his hand and leapt to his feet. "Harm! How are you doing? They wouldn't let me see you."

"I'm all right."

"I'm so sorry. This is all my fault. I'm such a fool."

"Don't worry about it."

"We thought you were dead."

"So did I."

"I have to change my ways. I *am* changing my ways."

Harm looked at the cards. "Still gambling, though."

"No way," said Kees. "I told you, I've changed. Besides, it takes two hands to gamble—one to hold the cards and one to rake in the money." He held up his left arm, his sleeve tied in a knot just below the elbow.

Harm gaped at the sleeve.

Kees grinned. "Now I play whist."

"Well, something good came of it, then."

"I'll never forget it. I saw that pinch-faced rebel pull the trigger. I saw you fall. I just knew you were dead. I tried to get your coat off you, but I couldn't. Ted got it open, and we saw that plate. I still thought you were dead. You wouldn't wake up."

"I'm awake now."

"I thank God every day," said Kees. "I mean, I thought I prayed before, but not like this. Now I know what prayer is."

Harm nodded. Spending a week in a hospital bed had taught him a few things about prayer as well. "What now?" he asked. "Will they send you home?"

"They want to, but I won't go. We have to see this thing through."

"Major Harrod wants to throw you in the stockade."

"Colonel Moore won't let him. Not after he heard I was first to the colors at Fort Anderson. I might have let that slip."

Ted visited the hospital every few days. Those were good days. He kept Harm and Kees updated on the progress of the war.

One day, Harm asked Ted why Gerrit hadn't visited.

"I invite him every time," said Ted. "He always has some excuse. Truth is, he's been acting strange ever since that night."

The next time Ted visited, Gerrit came with him.

"What took you so long?" teased Harm. "You got a girlfriend, or something?"

Gerrit was in no mood for joking.

"Sorry," said Harm. "I was hoping you'd read a psalm with me."

Gerrit looked uncomfortable. "Sorry. I forgot my Bible." He stayed for a bit, then excused himself, saying he needed to get back to camp.

Ted met Harm's glance. "Like I said, strange."

"He's angry at me," said Kees. "He has every right to be."

"I don't know," said Harm. "He seemed upset with *me*."

166

Later, when Ted turned to go, Kees stopped him. "Did you return those combs to the parsonage for me?"

"Sorry. I tried. But Colonel Moore won't let anyone out of camp."

Kees sighed. "I guess I'll have to return them myself—even if I have to do it after the war."

## CHAPTER 45

# MAY 1865

Golden-green leaves shimmered in the sun as a warm breeze swept through the trees surrounding the van Wyke home and farm.

Father joined Sam in the fields, grateful for a full recovery and a return to strength. In her garden, Mother admired her tulips, taking special pleasure in the red, yellow, and orange varieties she and Trina had planted the previous autumn.

Late in the day, Father went to town, and after supper they gathered to read the most recent letter from Harm.

———

Wilmington, North Carolina
April 24, 1865

Dear Father, Mother, and family at home,

The war is over! I'm sure you know by now of General Lee's surrender to General Grant at Appomattox Court House. We threw our caps into the air and gave a mighty shout when we heard the news. There was much celebrating.

Then, almost overnight, the news of President Lincoln's assassination. Such a shock. Such grief. Our joy is turned to mourning.

---

"Just like here," said Sam.

They all nodded in recognition. The entire town of Holland had been hit hard by the news that the president who'd led the Union to victory had been cut down. Black crepe paper had been hung from all the doors in town, even the church. The *dominie's* voice had trembled with emotion at the special worship service.

---

Mother, now that General Johnston has surrendered to General Sherman, it can't be long before they send us home.

Father, what a blessing you were able to pick up Mr. Brouwer's eighty acres. And at a good price. I believe it's good land, too.

Sam, now that we control the Cape Fear River, the engineers have built a pontoon bridge across it. I drew a picture for you. It is much like the one we crossed when we first arrived in Louisville.

---

Father examined the picture. "I've read about these, but never been able to picture them before." He passed it on to Sam.

---

Trina, a frequent sight in Wilmington is something they call Spanish moss. It hangs in clumps from the branches of the live oaks. Kees says it looks like an old man's beard.

I'm happy to report that I've fully recovered from my injury. Kees is also doing well. The rest of the regiment moved on to Salisbury, where they are to dismantle a prison camp. Kees and I remain in the hospital in Wilmington.

I pray that our long separation will soon come to an end. As always, we await God's will.

Your loving son and brother, Harm VanWyke

---

"When will he come home?" asked Trina.

"Maybe a month," said Father. "Maybe two."

"We should put in some of the new acreage," said Sam. "We'll have Harm to help with the harvest."

Father nodded. "That's good thinking."

Later, Father and Mother sat alone on the porch, enjoying the mild weather. After a bit, he said, "You're quiet tonight."

"I know. I'm just . . ." She paused, struggling to express her feelings. "I'm just filled with so much joy and longing and fear and gratitude—I don't think I can put it into words."

He nodded. He understood completely.

## CHAPTER 46

# MAY – JUNE 1865

Harm spent the last months of the war recuperating at the hospital in Wilmington. He used the time to consider his future beyond the war. His thoughts always returned to Sarah. Yes, whatever his future held, he knew it would include Sarah Tillema.

But everything else was unclear. God had spared him through many dangers, and he wanted his life to show the gratitude he felt in his heart. He wanted to be of service in his family, his church, his community and the Union he'd fought so hard to defend. But how?

And what about Yale? It was a rare opportunity to continue to learn, to grow. But he'd have to be away from home and family and church for several more years. Could he ask Sarah to make that sacrifice? And could he remain faithful in a community that sought to undermine and attack his faith, rather than build it up?

Harm asked Kees, "Have you heard from Susanna?"

"Susanna," Kees snorted. "She can have old Melvin Moerdyke if she wants him."

"Are you planning to go west then?"

"West?"

"Fighting Indians and all that."

Kees snorted again. "That's Major Harrod talking. I told him a long time ago, I'm not interested. I *like* Indians. I learned to fish from old grandfather Crofoot back home."

Harm smiled. That was good to hear.

"Don't worry about me." Kees grinned. "Put me on the first transport home. I can't wait to give Rev. van Raalte a big one-armed hug."

In May, they received two months' pay. Harm and Kees visited the hawkers' tents one last time. Kees bought a sword. He couldn't say why. Harm bought a sack of colorful seashells for Trina, a sugar bowl for his mother, and a necklace for Sarah.

In June, they were reunited with their regiment. Harm and his friends held one last time of devotions together. Gerrit didn't feel well and wasn't able to attend. Willem didn't make it either. The others gathered and sang Psalm 25:

*Unto me, O Lord Jehovah,*
*Show thy ways and teach thou me;*
*So that, by thy Spirit guided,*
*Clearly I thy paths may see.*

*In thy truth wilt thou me guide,*
*Teach me, God of my salvation;*
*All the day for thee I bide,*
*Lord, with eager expectation.*

Kees read Colossians 3, focusing on verses 23 and 24: *"And whatsoever ye do, do it heartily, as to the Lord, and not unto men; knowing that of the Lord ye shall receive the reward of the inheritance: for ye serve the Lord Christ."*

"I read that because we'll be starting over when we get home.

God spared our lives through an awful war. Now we have to figure out how to live that life."

"Any wisdom to share?" asked Harm.

Kees chucked. "I don't get that question a lot."

"Well?"

"Being a minister seems like a high calling," said Kees. "If I had Gerrit's smarts, that's what I'd do. But we each have different strengths."

"And interests," said Ted.

"I've got lots of interests," said Harm, "but they won't all pay the bills. We have to take into account our responsibilities, too."

Ted nodded. "And our circumstances."

"We can't let circumstances stand in our way, though," said Kees. "I've only got one arm, but I'm not going to let that stop me."

"Unless you want to be a juggler," said Ted.

Kees laughed. "Right. I see your point. No circus for me."

"Our circumstances do enter in," agreed Harm. "Old Mr. Visser has that sister he takes care of. He couldn't very well take a job in Kalamazoo or Grand Haven."

"Like Kees said, we should use our God-given abilities," said Ted. "He gave Gerrit a mind to read and study. He gave Kees a mind for business."

"How about me?" asked Harm. "What's my unique ability?"

Kees grinned. "Identifying trees at a hundred paces."

Later, when they'd turned in for the night, Harm was too restless to sleep. His future was still shrouded in mist. Identifying trees wouldn't exactly put food on the table.

The next morning, as Harm was packing his things away, Spencer and Clay came to visit him one last time. "My father wants to know if you're still interested in Yale."

Harm sighed. "I've decided against it."

Spencer didn't seem surprised. "I was afraid you might tell me that."

"I appreciate the offer. It's very generous. And tempting. But I've decided to go back home."

"Your parents have something against college?"

"That's not it," said Harm. "I never even told them."

"Why then?"

"I want to learn everything there is to know about this creation—how things grow, how they develop, how each little thing affects every other thing. I have so many questions. But I want to understand things as they truly are. Explanations that exclude or ignore God—that just seems like foolishness."

"You don't have to believe everything they teach," said Spencer. "I didn't."

"I know. I'm sure some people could benefit from it. But not me. Not now."

"What will you do back home?"

"Probably help my father on the farm at first, try to save up some money. There's a Dutch Reformed college back east called Rutgers. It probably won't happen, but I don't want to rule anything out yet."

Harm carefully stored the package with the necklace for Sarah in with his things. Yes, his future included her as well. He turned back to Spencer. "How about you? What will you do after the war?"

"I'm a bit unsure, myself," answered Spencer.

"You could come to Holland."

Spencer grinned. "My Dutch isn't that good. To be honest, I've been thinking I might go back east, try to re-establish a relationship with my family."

"I thought they were hypocrites."

"I accused them of that. Yeah. But that was probably unfair. They're just imperfect, like everyone else."

Harm considered that answer. It showed a lot of maturity. He hoped he could show the same humility when it came to facing his own parents. But first, he had one more question for Spencer. "What about your relationship with God?"

Spencer smiled. "I think of that sometimes. I suppose I have you to blame for that."

"There's nothing more important."

"I know you believe that."

Harm extended his hand. "I'll pray for you."

Spencer took his hand. "Have a good life, Harm."

Clay remained after Spencer left. Harm asked him, "What will you do now? You can't go back to living on the streets."

"I won't."

"I can find a place for you in Holland. You could work on a farm or get a job in town."

"Thank you. You're the third person to offer to help me."

"That's great. Who else?"

"Spencer, for one. He said I could go east with him and stay with his family as long as I wanted."

Harm was relieved that one way or another, Clay would be all right. They shook hands, and Harm wished him well.

On June 24, the 25th Michigan Volunteer Infantry mustered out of the U.S. Army, and talk turned to their return home.

Willem stopped to see Harm. "Looking forward to getting home?"

"Very much."

"It might not be like you remember it."

"I'm sure it won't be."

"It'll seem awfully backwards after seeing the world."

"Maybe. But we can get to work on the things we talked about—a better harbor, a railroad, industry."

"Still, in the end, Holland will be just another insignificant town."

"Maybe. But it will be *our* insignificant town."

"There are other options," said Willem. "Major Harrod is still looking for people to join him in the war department."

Harm wasn't impressed. "Major Harrod is a snake."

"He does whatever it takes," said Willem. "I admire him."

"Enough to join the war department?"

"Yes, actually. I leave for Washington tomorrow."

Harm stared at him, unsure what to say. He wanted to be shocked, but realized he'd seen this coming for a long time.

Willem grabbed him by the arm. "Join us. We'll be in the capitol, where all the action is."

"What about Holland?"

"Face it, Holland is old-fashioned. It always will be. I'm getting out. You should, too."

"What about church?"

"I'll still go to church when I can." He dropped his eyes. "I'll be traveling a lot."

"Church is important," said Harm.

"I know. But I don't think it should stand in the way of doing what we want in life."

Harm cringed. That sounded a lot like Spencer. "Have you talked with your parents?"

"I'm through listening to other people." Willem's voice took on an edge of anger. "From now on, I do what I want." He turned on his heel and left.

Harm felt numb. He'd seen this coming. But he hadn't done anything to stop it. He hadn't done enough. Guilt washed over him. How could he face Uncle Ben and Aunt Nel?

## CHAPTER 47

# JUNE 1865

When June came to an end, the 25th Michigan struck tents and packed everything for their return home.

As Harm and his friends stood at the railroad station waiting for transports to arrive, Kees asked Harm, "Have you decided what you're going to do when we get home?"

"My father just bought eighty acres from Mr. Brouwer," said Harm. "I guess I'll help him with that."

Kees chuckled. "Try not to sound so excited."

"I can't complain. It's a good life."

Harm turned to Gerrit. "How about you, Gerrit, what are you going to do when we get home?"

Gerrit didn't answer.

"He's going to be the new preacher," said Kees. "Everyone knows that."

"You don't know anything," snapped Gerrit. He stalked off without even stopping to gather his gear.

Kees looked at Harm, "What did I say?"

Ted said, "He's still upset about that thing at the parsonage."

Kees nodded. "I deserve that, then. But I don't know how to make it up to him."

"Let me talk to him," said Harm.

He followed after Gerrit. When he caught up to him, he said, "I want to apologize."

Gerrit looked up. "You? For what?"

"When we joined the infantry, we talked about walking faithfully, even as soldiers. I haven't always done that. And when others didn't, I let you take the heat for pointing it out. That was pretty rotten."

Gerrit looked away. "You don't need to apologize for anything."

"I do. I'm sorry. I hope you can forgive me. I know you don't want to hear it, but Kees is sorry, too. I hope someday you can forgive us."

Gerrit didn't respond. Harm didn't know what else to say. He returned to Kees and Ted.

"What did he say?" asked Kees.

"Not much."

They waited in silence for some time, then Kees asked, "So, what would you do if you could do anything in the world?"

"Eat a really good peach?" said Ted.

Kees laughed. "We just won a war. Think big."

Harm sighed. "If things were different, I wish I could continue my education."

"More schooling? That's the *last* thing I'd want."

"There's so much to learn, though."

"And yet you turned down Yale."

"I hope I don't live to regret that."

"Sounds to me like you want to be a preacher." Kees grinned. "Maybe that's why Gerrit's upset."

Harm smiled, but shook his head. "There's nothing more important than preaching God's word, but God speaks in creation, too—stars and trees and birds, even art and music. Things the Belgic Confession calls "a most elegant book." I want to help people see God's hand in those things."

"A teacher, then."

Harm sighed. "If I could do anything, sure, but I've got to consider my circumstances, right? I'll work on the farm and see what happens. If that's all I ever do, I want to do it with all my heart, as unto the Lord."

"A teacher, then."

Harm ignored him. "How about you? What do you want to do?"

"I'll tell you what I *don't* want," said Kees. "I don't want to work in my father's warehouse."

"What then?"

"I've got circumstances, too." He raised his left arm. "This limits my options."

"Does it hurt?"

"Only my pride."

"You're not angry?"

"At who? Bushwhackers? Maybe. God? No. You may not have noticed, but I can be thick-headed sometimes. Slow to learn a lesson. Gerrit tried to teach me. You tried. Finally, God used a language I can't ignore. If your right hand offends you, cut it off. In my case it was the left arm, but you get the idea." He raised his arm again. "Proof God doesn't wink at sin."

"Is that from the Bible?" asked Ted. "Wink at sin?"

"I don't know," said Harm.

"I think it's in Romans. Who's got a Bible?" Kees spotted Gerrit's haversack and dug through it. He pulled out a red leather book with gold letters, a Greek New Testament. "What's this?" He pulled out more books.

Harm recognized them, and shoved them back into Gerrit's haversack.

Kees recognized them, too. "Oh, this is good. Where is he?"

"Don't," said Harm.

"I've been waiting for this my whole life."

"Don't."

Kees looked at Harm. "He's such a hypocrite. Don't tell me you're going to let him get away with this."

"*This* is what's been bothering him," said Harm. "Let me talk to him."

"Let *me* talk to him," said Kees.

"*I'll* talk to him," said Harm.

Kees sighed. "All right. But I get to listen."

Gerrit saw them coming. Before Harm could say anything, he said, "What would you do if Rev. van Raalte turned out to be a fraud?"

Ted raised an eyebrow. "You know something we don't?"

Gerrit shook his head. "I'm sorry. I have something I have to tell you."

"Go ahead," said Harm.

"It's so shameful." He looked around. "Where's my haversack? I have to show you something."

"This haversack?" Kees held it up.

"Look inside."

"We already have."

Gerrit hung his head. "I stole a Bible from a church."

"A parsonage, technically," said Ted.

"What does that make me?"

"A person who falls into sin," said Harm. "Like the rest of us."

"It's humiliating."

"It's humbling."

"I've wanted to be a minister my whole life. And now, that's impossible."

"Is it?" said Harm.

"Who wants a minister who's capable of that?"

"I'd only want a minister who knows he's capable of that," replied Kees.

"I'm sorry I've been treating everybody poorly." Gerrit buried his face in his hands. "I wanted to return them and beg the minister to forgive me. Colonel Moore wouldn't let me out of camp."

"I'll be making a return trip to that parsonage after the dust settles," said Kees. "I can take them back for you."

Gerrit shook his head. "I have to do it myself. But if you'll have me, I'll go with you."

## CHAPTER 48

# JUNE – JULY 1865

The transports brought the 25th Michigan to Jackson, Michigan, where they received their final pay and were formally discharged from the infantry. From there, they continued on to Kalamazoo.

Kees' father met them at the railroad station in Kalamazoo. He hugged Kees, stood back to look at him, then hugged him again.

He shook hands with Harm. "I can't believe it. You were boys when you left."

He moved on to Ted. "Ted, I'm so sorry about your father."

After greeting everyone, Kees' father said, "I want you to know I've got jobs for anyone who wants one, *everyone* who wants one."

Rinze Rietema said, "That's kind of you, Mr. de Groot."

"Not at all," insisted Mr. de Groot. "It's business. You're the best crop of talent our town is likely to produce."

Only Kees seemed unimpressed. "Seems a shame to bury all that talent in your warehouse."

"Warehouse?!" said Mr. de Groot. "Listen, I have ten businesses going and fifty more in my head. Don't like leatherworks? I can use you in my lumbermill. Don't like lumber? How about windmills?"

"Windmills?" said Kees. "That's a new one."

"Don't laugh. Folks are moving west. They're building home-steads in the Great American Desert. How do they water their crops? How do they water their stock? Windmills! Who knows windmills better than the Dutch? I'm selling them faster than I can build them. I need a production manager. I need someone to oversee delivery."

Kees perked up. "That could be fun."

Mr. de Groot had arranged for a line of wagons to take the boys back to Holland. A gentle breeze fluttered the trees, and the "white glove regiment" fairly quivered with anticipation. The sky stretched overhead as blue as Lake Michigan in the morning. Some of the boys slept. Some talked together. Harm sat quietly in the last wagon, lost in his own thoughts.

As they approached Holland, they passed the cemetery. Harm slipped off from the wagon. He watched as the others continued on without him, then turned to the cemetery. It was larger than when he'd left. They'd opened a whole new section. On the newer grave markers, he saw the names of people who'd been alive and well when he left.

Someone had recently cleared the area around Jacob's grave and left fresh flowers. Harm traced the name on the stone. He expected the old sadness to return, but felt only gratitude. Jacob had completed his work and gone to glory. He had served God and his neighbor and taught Harm important lessons about mak-ing the most of life. Now, it was Harm's turn to take up the work, whatever that might be.

He turned to go, but noticed another figure in the newer sec-tion of the cemetery. He walked over to join him.

"I saw you slip off the wagon," said Ted. "I thought I should pay my respects as well." He hunched down and brushed a leaf from the stone that marked his father's grave. "I could have been a better son."

"You and me both."

They turned toward town and walked the last few miles together.

"What's it going to be?" asked Harm. "Leatherworks, lumberyard, windmills?"

Ted smiled. "I'm a landowner. I think I'd like to farm."

"Sounds great. You might want to find a hired hand, though. It's a lot of work for one man."

"It's already arranged."

"Yeah?"

Ted grinned. "Clay."

When they approached the city, Harm marveled at the changes. Buildings had sprung up where empty fields had lain. Holland had grown into a thriving, bustling town. It looked like a hundred other towns they'd marched through, except for the Dutch language that could still be heard in the streets. As they ran into people they knew, they heard familiar Dutch greetings: *Hallo, Welkom thuis,* and *God zij dank.*

Harm had become so accustomed to speaking English that returning to Holland felt almost as strange as it had felt to leave three years earlier.

A throng of people were gathered on the town square. Tears of joy flowed as soldiers were reunited with their families. Tears of sorrow, too. Otto Boot's family stood among the crowd. Harm realized how hard it must be for them, knowing they would have to wait for their glad reunion day in glory.

Harm scanned the crowd for his family. He spotted Uncle Ben and Aunt Nel standing alone. He walked over to join them. Aunt Nel clung to him and wouldn't let go. He clung to her, too, but couldn't bring himself to look her in the eyes. Uncle Ben shook his hand awkwardly, "We'll talk, yes?"

"Of course," said Harm, stabbed with regret. He should have pushed Willem to attend devotions more often. He should have shielded him from Spencer's influence. He would have to carry the burden of that failure his whole life.

"Harm!"

He turned to see Henry and Anna. She rushed into his arms and held him tight. Henry held little Eliza, almost three years old, by one hand and a newborn baby with the other.

Eliza tugged at Harm's coat. "Welcome 'ome, Uncle 'arm."

Harm shifted his gear and took Eliza up in his arms. "Thank you, Eliza. I'm glad to be home."

She reached for his cap. He took it off and placed it on her head.

She giggled. "I can't see."

He tilted the cap back. "Better?"

"Better."

Harm turned his gaze to his new nephew. "He's beautiful."

Anna smiled. "He's eleven days today. Do you want to hold him?"

Harm set Eliza back on the ground and took the baby in his arms.

"We called him Jacob," said Anna.

Harm's voice caught in his throat. "It's a good name."

"Father wanted to come," said Anna, "but Lottie is about to have a calf and it looks to be a difficult delivery. Mother stayed with him. They'll see you at the house."

Harm looked for Sarah Tillema, but didn't see her in the crowd. The loss of Howard would make this hard for her family. Perhaps they'd remained home. He noticed Melvin Moerdyke strutting through the crowd with Susanna on his arm. He excused himself and sought out Kees to try to head off trouble. But if Kees had noticed, he was taking it well. He stood in the shade of a great oak tree, talking quietly with Gerrit's younger sister, Nellie Bol.

Beyond the square, Harm looked toward the church standing guard over the town. For the first time, he noticed how much taller it stood than the other buildings. Its pillars and windows and bell tower all seemed to draw the mind heavenward. He'd never realized how architecture could influence the spirit. It was the kind of thing he might have studied at Yale.

He had a sudden urge to visit the church. He turned in that direction, then stopped as he spotted Sarah. She walked toward him looking more lovely than ever, her dark hair glistening in the sunlight. Her eyes shone and a smile parted her lips.

Harm moved toward her and took her into his arms. He swung her once around before setting her down again. He was aware others were watching, but didn't care. He looked into her eyes and they embraced again.

When they finally parted, he said, "It's so good to see you again."

She said something but it was lost in the din of the celebration.

He told her he'd like to walk over by the church building. "Will you come with me?"

She smiled and took his arm.

They found the *dominie* leaning against one of the pillars. "Welcome home, Harm."

"Rev. van Raalte! What are you doing here? I thought you'd be over on the square with everyone else."

"I've just come from meeting with some of the families who grieve the loss of loved ones." He turned to Sarah, "My sympathies to you, once more."

She nodded almost imperceptibly and squeezed Harm's arm tighter.

He turned to Harm. "I'd like to show you something."

He led Harm and Sarah to the top of the bell tower and pointed out a fine three-story brick building across the way. "Our little Academy is expanding. We'll call it Hope College. We'll train the next generation of ministers and teachers right here in Holland."

"What a blessing for the parents, to have their children instructed by faithful teachers and preachers," said Harm.

"My thoughts exactly," said the *dominie*. He drew his watch from his vest pocket and raised an eyebrow. "Time for us to get back to the festivities. I believe I'm supposed to make some remarks."

Harm took Sarah's hand. "We'll be along in a bit."

When they returned to the square, the first faces Harm saw were Sam and Trina. Sam's blond hair was bleached nearly white from the sun. He was no longer a scrawny sixteen-year-old. His shoulders were square, his face and arms were bronzed. They embraced, and Sam slapped him on the back.

Trina wedged herself into the hug—older, but still impatient. She had grown tall and slender, with bright eyes and a quick smile.

Harm reached into his haversack and produced her gift, carefully wrapped. She pulled away the paper, revealing the shells. "From the ocean?"

He nodded. "There are different kinds. This is a Scotch bonnet. That's a whelk. These pointy ones are augers. The flat ones are scallops. The big one is a conch."

She fingered the shells, then hugged Harm again. "I wish we had an ocean."

Rev. van Raalte took the stage, and everyone quieted down to hear his remarks. He congratulated the boys on their achievement, calling to remembrance their victory against all odds at the battle at Tebbs Bend on the Green River. He led everyone in the singing of a psalm and offered a prayer of gratitude for their safe return.

The celebration continued long after Rev. van Raalte's remarks, but Harm was eager to see his parents again. He finally parted with Sarah and headed across the fields toward home.

As soon as he came within sight of the house, his mother ran out to meet him. Her shoulders shook as she hugged him. "Come. Father is in the barn." They hugged again, then continued on toward the house.

As Harm entered the yard, his father stepped out from the barn. He looked older than when Harm had left, but not *so* old.

"Hello, Father."

"Welcome home, son."

They embraced. Harm clung to him, fighting back tears.

"I'm sorry I couldn't be in town," said his father.

"It's all right," said Harm. "How's Lottie?"

"Fine. Just fine. Come see." He led Harm to the barn. Lottie lay on her side, contentedly watching her newborn calf as it sucked greedily.

Harm smiled. He'd seen enough of death. It was good to see new life.

"Have you seen the *dominie*?" asked his father.

"I have. He showed me the new college."

"He has high hopes for it. We all do. The *dominie* . . . he thinks you'd make a good school teacher. He thinks you'd like that."

Harm looked up in surprise. "I would, but . . ."

His father's face held a look of wonderment. "I never imagined a child of mine could be a school teacher."

"But . . . we could never afford it."

"We've saved every dollar you sent home. And we've done

some extras. Sam opened up the back pasture. We planted fruit trees. We even keep bees now."

They went inside the house and Harm's mother poured coffee. His father looked suddenly grave. "You've seen the world."

Harm nodded.

"You've encountered the lie."

"I have," said Harm. He picked up his father's *Bijbel* from the counter and laid it on the table. "But I love the truth."

His father reached into Harm's haversack and laid his English Bible next to his own. "I am a child of the old country, I suppose. And you are a child of the new. But there is one truth."

They embraced again.

"Amen."

# Afterword

**H**istorical fiction presents a number of challenges, one of which is how to weave historical events into a fictional story. Much of this book is based on historical events. The 25th Michigan was formed in Kalamazoo and moved by rail to Louisville, where they took part in funeral ceremonies and provost duties. They battled General John Hunt Morgan at Tebbs Bend on the Green River, marched 200 miles to East Tennessee, battled Confederate troops around Knoxville, and took part in General Sherman's advance on Atlanta. They fought at Franklin and Nashville in Tennessee, traveled by steamboat to the nation's capital, and closed out the war in North Carolina.

I have tried to portray the history in harmony with the available research. But while the book is true to history as much as possible, it is not a history book. It is a work of fiction. As such, I have on occasion altered events and timelines in the interest of telling a good story.

Another challenge is how to flesh out historical figures beyond what is available in the historical record. Rev. Albertus C. van Raalte, Colonel Orlando Moore, and Captain Martin de Boe, among others in this story, were real people. Again, I have sought to portray them in harmony with the available research. Firsthand accounts relate that Rev. van Raalte was an ardent supporter of sending the young men of the *Kolonie* to fight in the war. Colonel Moore, according to his contemporaries, showed deep concern for his soldiers and great skill in preparing his regiment for battle. Still, as to their specific words and actions in this story, I have had to rely on my imagination.

Several of the soldiers mentioned in this story died in the course of their service. These include Arie Rot, William Dowd, Pieter ver Shure, Cornelius van Dam, and Otto Boot. Due to limited historical information about them, I have had to present their dialogue and family backgrounds in a fictional way.

In some cases, I have chosen to substitute fictional characters for their historical counterparts. The 25th Michigan did have a major, a chaplain, and a bugler, but Major Harrod, Rev. Mann, and Spencer Grey are entirely fictional characters.

The main characters in the story—Harm, Ted, Kees, Gerrit, Willem, Howard, and Sarah—along with their various family members are all fictional.

In developing this book, I have benefited greatly from a number of organizations devoted to keeping history alive including the following:

1. Bentley Historical Library on the campus of the University of Michigan, which holds the Civil War letters of Charles Woodruff, a soldier from Niles, Michigan, as well as regular dispatches from Asa W. Slayton, which were published in the *Grand Rapids Weekly Eagle.*
2. Calvin University and Calvin Theological Seminary Archives, located in Heritage Hall in the Hekman Library of Calvin University, which publish *Origins, Historical Magazine of The Ar-*

*chives,* and hold many of the papers of Rev. van Raalte and his family.

3. Joint Archives of Holland, located in the Theil Research Center, which publishes *The Joint Archives Quarterly* and holds numerous resources related to the early days of the Holland colony.

4. The Holland Museum, which houses historical artifacts associated with Company I of the 25th Michigan.

For insight into the daily joys and sorrows experienced by soldiers from Holland in the Civil War, I have relied heavily on compiled letters of soldiers from Holland who volunteered in the 25th Michigan, especially *The Civil War Letters of Johannes Van Lente,* and *My Country and Cross: The Civil War Letters of John Anthony Wilterdink Company I, 25th Michigan Infantry.*

Other helpful resources include *The Story of the Twenty-fifth Michigan,* by Benjamin F. Travis, a lieutenant who served in the regiment, and *A Bend in the River,* by Terry VandeWater, a fact-based account of the 25th Michigan through its battle with General John Hunt Morgan's raiders at Tebbs Bend on the Green River.

For those interested in more information about the 25th Michigan, I recommend the following resources, from which I have benefited:

## Books

Jacobson, Jeanne M., Elton J. Bruins, and Larry J. Wagenaar. *Albertus C. VanRaalte: Dutch Leader and American Patriot.* Joint Archives of Holland, 2001.

Lente, Johannes Van, and Van Lente Janice L. *The Civil War Let-*

*ters of Johannes Van Lente*. Okemos, MI: Yankee Girl Publications, 1995.

Schoolland, Marian M. *De Kolonie: The Church That God Transplanted*. Grand Rapids, MI: Board of Publications of the Christian Reformed Church, 1974.

Swierenga, Robert P. *Holland Michigan: From Dutch Colony to Dynamic City*. Holland, MI: Van Raalte Press, 2014.

Travis, Benjamin F. *The Story of the Twenty-Fifth Michigan*. Nabu Press, 2012.

VandeWater, Terry. *A Bend in the River*. Bloomington, IN: AuthorHouse, 2005.

Wilterdink, John Anthony, and Albert H. McGeehan. *My Country and Cross: the Civil War Letters of John Anthony Wilterdink, Company I, 25th Michigan Infantry*, 1982.


## Pamphlet

Boonstra, Harry, and Michael De Vries. *Pillar Church in the Van Raalte Era*. Pillar Christian Reformed Church, 2003.


## Articles

Brinks, H.J. "Dutch American Reactions." *Origins* VI, no. 1 (1988).
Jacobs, Christine. "Avoiding the War." *Origins* VI, no. 1 (1988).
"Rev. A. C. Van Raalte on Slavery." Translated by Michael Douma. *Origins* XXXI, no. 2 (2013).

# Military Terms

## ARMY UNITS

Company
: The basic unit of warfare, approximately one hundred soldiers

Regiment
: Composed of a number of companies, usually ten

Brigade
: Composed of a number of regiments, usually three to five

Division
: Composed of a number of brigades, usually three to five

Corps
: Composed of a number of divisions, usually three

Army
: Composed of a number of corps, from one to eight

## ARMY RANKS

Private
: A soldier of the lowest military rank

Lieutenant
: An officer second in command of a company

Captain
: An officer in command of a company

Major
: An officer second in command of a regiment

Colonel
: An officer in command of a regiment

General | Highest ranking officer, usually in command of a division, corps, or army

## BUGLE CALLS

Reveille | A bugle call played to mark the beginning of the day

Tattoo | A bugle call played in the evening, generally half an hour before lights out

Taps | A bugle call played to mark the end of the day

## OTHER MILITARY TERMS

Artillery | Large-caliber guns, cannons

Bayonet | A blade affixed to a musket for use in hand-to-hand fighting

Colors | Flags of the Union, Confederacy, state, and regiment carried on the march and in battle

Drill | Regular, often rigorous training of soldiers for their duties, such as battle tactics and formations

Flank | The right or left edge or wing of a military unit or position

Flanking Movement | To move around and gain the edge or wing of an enemy, avoiding a frontal assault

Forage | Unauthorized seizing of food or provisions, usually from neighboring homes and farms

Latrine | A pit designated for use as a toilet

Musket | A muzzle-loading firearm

Picket | A soldier posted outside of camp to give early warning of approaching forces

Picket Line   A line of picket posts surrounding a camp to give early warning of approaching forces

Quartermaster An officer responsible for providing soldiers with food, clothing, weapons, and other supplies

Skirmish      A minor battle, often connected to or leading to a larger battle

Skirmish Line A number of soldiers spread out in a line, in advance of a larger fighting force

Sutler        Non-military person authorized to sell supplies to soldiers near a military camp

# Civil War Timeline

| 25th Michigan | 1861 | Larger War |
| --- | --- | --- |
| | January | Several southern states secede from the Union |
| | February | Confederate States of America formed |
| | March | Abraham Lincoln inaugurated to the United States presidency |
| | April | Confederate forces fire on Fort Sumter |
| | May | The Secession Convention meets in Raleigh, North Carolina |
| | June | Union and Confederate forces skirmish in Virginia |
| | July | First battle of Manassas (also known as Bull Run) in Virginia |
| | August | Monthly pay for an Army private raised to $13 |
| | September | General Polk tries to take Kentucky for the Confederacy |
| | October | Blockade of southern ports causes shortages |

| 25th Michigan | 1862 | Larger War |
|---|---|---|
| | November | An old factory in Salisbury, North Carolina, becomes a prison camp |
| | December | Union and Confederate forces skirmish in Kentucky |
| | January | The Union's first ironclad, the USS Monitor, is launched |
| | February | Confederates surrender to General Grant at Fort Donelson, Tennessee |
| | March | *USS Monitor* battles Confederate ironclad, *CSS Virginia* (also known as *Merrimack*) |
| | April | Battle of Shiloh in Tennessee |
| | May | Union General Bunjamin Butler occupies New Orleans |
| | June | Battle of Fair Oaks in Virginia |
| | July | The bugle call taps is first played as a call to extinguish lights |
| Volunteers from Holland, Michigan, leave home for Kalamazoo, Michigan | August | The Second Battle of Manassas (also known as Bull Run) in Virginia |
| 25th Michigan Volunteer Infantry Regiment is organized | September | Battle of Antietam (also known as Sharpsburg) in Maryland |
| 25th Michigan boards transports for Louisville, Kentucky | October | Battle of Perryville in Kentucky |
| | November | President Lincoln fires General George McClellan |
| First skirmish with rebel raider, General John Hunt Morgan | December | Battle of Fredericksburg in Virginia |
| 25th Michigan | 1863 | Larger War |
| | January | Emancipation Proclamation goes into effect |
| | February | |

198

| 25th Michigan | | Larger War |
|---|---|---|
| | March | President Lincoln offers amnesty to Union deserters if they will return to their units |
| | April | The first United States draft takes effect |
| | May | Battle of Chancellorsville in Virginia |
| | June | Siege of Vicksburg |
| Battle at Tebbs Bend on the Green River | July | Battle of Gettysburg, fall of Vicksburg |
| Long march from western Kentucky to east Tennessee | August | Union Army of the Cumberland begins Chickamauga campaign in east Tennessee |
| Arrive in Knoxville, Tennessee | September | Battle of Chickamauga in Tennessee |
| Skirmishes around Knoxville | October | General Grant moves to reinforce Chattanooga |
| Battle at Mossy Creek | November | Battle of Chattanooga |
| | December | Confederate siege of Knoxville ends |
| **25th Michigan** | **1864** | **Larger War** |
| | January | |
| | February | Captured Union soldiers are placed in the prison at Andersonville, Georgia |
| | March | President Lincoln makes General Grant commander of all Union armies |
| | April | General Grant discountinues the practice of exchanging prisoners of war |
| Battle of Rocky Face Ridge and Resaca, Georgia, among others | May | Battle of the Wilderness in Virginia |
| Almost daily battles, including Pine Mountain, Lost Mountain, and Kennesaw Mountain | June | Battle of Cold Harbor in Viriginia |

| Arrive in Atlanta | July | Confederate General John Bell Hood put in charge of defending Atlanta, Georgia |
| Battle of Utoy Creek | August | Former Union General George B. McClellan becomes Democratic candidate for president |
| Atlanta falls | September | General Sherman takes Atlanta, Georgia |
| | October | Union General Philip Sheridan cuts a path through the rich Shenandoah Valley |
| Battle of Franklin, Tennessee | November | President Lincoln is re-elected, General Hood marches toward Nashville |
| Battle at Nashville, Tennessee | December | General Sherman takes Savannah, Georgia; General Hood is defeated at Nashville |

| 25th Michigan | 1865 | Larger War |
| --- | --- | --- |
| Travel east to Washington via steamship and railroad | January | Fort Fisher at the mouth of the Cape Fear River in North Carolina falls to Union troops |
| Travel by steamship to Cape Fear River, battle to take Fort Anderson | February | Wilmington, North Carolina, falls |
| | March | |
| Liberate prison camp at Salisbury, North Carolina | April | General Lee surrenders; six days later, President Lincoln is assassinated |
| | May | Jefferson Davis is captured at Irwinville, Georgia |
| Leave Salisbury for Jackson, Michigan | June | Union troops in Galveston, Texas, bring news the war is over |
| Arrive home in Holland, Michigan, to great celebration | July | |

# Musical Lyrics Credits

## Chapter 3

Psalm 73: William Kuipers, 1931, © Faith Alive Christian Resources. Used with permission.

Psalm 121: Dewey Westra, 1931, © Faith Alive Christian Resources. Used with permission.

## Chapter 5

Psalm 116: William Kuipers, 1931, © Faith Alive Christian Resources. Used with permission.

## Chapter 6

Psalm 19: William Helder, 2015, in the *New Genevan Psalter*, © William Helder. Used with permission.

## Chapter 12

Psalm 68: Benjamin Essenberg, 1931, © Faith Alive Christian Resources. Used with permission.

## Chapter 24

Shape note Psalm 42: 1991, © The Sacred Harp Publishing Company, Inc, Carrollton, GA, publishers of *The Sacred Harp*. Used with permission.

## Chapter 32

Psalm 119: Dewey Westra, 1931, © Faith Alive Christian Resources. Used with permission.

Psalm 27: William Helder, 2015, in the *New Genevan Psalter*, © William Helder. Used with permission.

## Chapter 33

Psalm 65: William Kuipers, 1931, © Faith Alive Christian Resources. Used with permission.

## Chapter 46

Psalm 25: Samuel G. Brondsema, 1931, © Faith Alive Christian Resources. Used with permission.

www.ingramcontent.com/pod-product-compliance
Lightning Source LLC
Chambersburg PA
CBHW070008260626
47159CB00005B/1726